WILMETTE PUBLIC LIBRARY

3 1239 00824 7832

D1058204

Wilmette Public Library
1242 Wilmette Avenue
Wilmette, Il 60091
847-256-5025

THE
BAD
KID

SARAH LARIVIERE

THE BAD KID

WITHDRAWN
Wilmette Public Library

SIMON & SCHUSTER BOOKS FOR YOUNG READERS
NEW YORK   LONDON   TORONTO   SYDNEY   NEW DELHI

WILMETTE PUBLIC LIBRARY
1242 WILMETTE AVENUE
WILMETTE, IL 60091
847-256-5025

SIMON & SCHUSTER BOOKS FOR YOUNG READERS
An imprint of Simon & Schuster Children's Publishing Division
1230 Avenue of the Americas, New York, New York 10020

This book is a work of fiction. Any references to historical events, real people,
or real places are used fictitiously. Other names, characters, places, and events are
products of the author's imagination, and any resemblance to actual events or
places or persons, living or dead, is entirely coincidental.
Text copyright © 2016 by Sarah Lariviere
Jacket illustration copyright © 2016 by Ziyue Chen
All rights reserved, including the right of reproduction in whole or in part in any form.

SIMON & SCHUSTER BOOKS FOR YOUNG READERS is a trademark of Simon & Schuster, Inc.
For information about special discounts for bulk purchases, please contact Simon & Schuster
Special Sales at 1-866-506-1949 or business@simonandschuster.com.
The Simon & Schuster Speakers Bureau can bring authors to your live event. For more
information or to book an event, contact the Simon & Schuster Speakers Bureau
at 1-866-248-3049 or visit our website at www.simonspeakers.com.
Interior design by Tom Daly
Jacket design by Laurent Linn
The text for this book was set in Adobe Garamond Pro.
Manufactured in the United States of America
0816 FFG
First Edition
2 4 6 8 10 9 7 5 3 1
Library of Congress Cataloging-in-Publication Data
Names: Lariviere, Sarah, author.
Title: The bad kid / Sarah Lariviere.
Description: First edition. | New York : Simon & Schuster Books for Young Readers, [2016] | Summary: In the Brooklyn
neighborhood of Sunset Park, eleven-year-old Claudeline Feng LeBernardin hopes to take over the "family business"
previously run by her mobster grandfather, who has recently passed away, while trying to uncover a local scam artist and
salvage her friendship with her best friend and partner in crime, Fingerless Brett.
Identifiers: LCCN 2015045427| ISBN 9781481435819 (hardback) | ISBN 9781481435840 (eBook)
Subjects: | CYAC: Gangsters—Fiction. | Families—Fiction. |
Friendship—Fiction. | Brooklyn (New York, N.Y.)—Fiction. | Mystery and
detective stories. | Humorous stories. | Racially mixed people—Fiction. |
BISAC: JUVENILE FICTION / Social Issues / New Experience. | JUVENILE
FICTION / Family / General (see also headings under Social Issues). |
JUVENILE FICTION / Social Issues / Friendship.
Classification: LCC PZ7.1.L345 Bad 2016 | DDC [Fic]—dc23
LC record available at https://lccn.loc.gov/2015045427

J
Lariviere

To my grandparents,
who taught me how to live

9/5/11

To my parents,
who taught me how to live

FINGERLESS BRETT

The good ones I declare good;
the bad ones I also declare good.
—Lao Tzu, philosopher

CACHINK! When the garden gnome smacked the bricks next to Fingerless Brett's bedroom window, I ducked. *Clunk. Clunk.* On the dirty sidewalk, busted gnome chunks sparkled in the sun. My aim must've been getting better. This time he pushed back his curtains after the first pitch. I gave him the four-fingered wave.

I've been trying to think up some new ways of describing my best friend, Fingerless Brett, besides that he walks around Brooklyn like a king penguin with a squinty eye and a missing finger. But that's exactly what he's looked like every day since he moved to the neighborhood a few years ago. It's the perfect way to describe him. Okay: He wears shoes. He wears a T-shirt and shorts, except if it's cold he wears a hoodie and pants. What else? He ain't too fat but he ain't skinny, either, which is why he's a king penguin instead of a regular one. I'll tell you something else if I think of it.

"Claudeline!" yelled Mother Fingerless, and in a New York minute she was in my face with the gnome chunks and the yadda yadda. There wouldn't have been any point trying to slip past her to get to Brett. She would've chased me upstairs with a salami and complained for a couple hours about kids like me and a life full of problems, and Brett and me never would've made it to the park. I've been down that alley before.

"You tell Claudeline," she said to Brett, who was coming up behind her, "she owes me a new statue. And if she steals it off our neighbor, I'm gonna know."

Brett took a gnome chunk from her hand. "He'll live, Ma. We've got glue."

"Just had to toughen him up a little bit," I said.

Mother Fingerless tugged the neck of her pink, flowered muumuu to make a breeze. Her black eyebrows and curly black hair are the same as Brett's, but her skin is olive-tan with beauty marks, and Brett's is deep, dark brown. She kept looking back and forth between Brett and me.

"What?" I said.

She turned to Brett. "I am over this bad kid today. Okay? She's got no supervision." Then she lifted her chin and gave me the once-over, like I was a grimy sidewalk that needed a good hosing down. "I'm gonna teach you how to be a young lady, Claudeline."

Brett put an arm around his mother's shoulders. "You tell her, Ma."

I stuck out my tongue at him.

"You be home before it's dark, Brett," said Mother Fingerless as she headed inside. "Claudeline, too, because I'm not going out to look for her tonight. Brett, you help me craft later; don't forget."

Brett blew her a kiss.

I yelled, "See ya tomorrow, young lady. Take it easy on the bonbons!" Then Brett and me headed up Sixtieth Street. There's more than one Sixtieth Street in New York City, and ours is in Sunset Park. Home of Brooklyn's very own Chinatown, my favorite place in the world. Not that I've got much to compare it to. But who needs other places when you're born into the best one on the first try?

I nudged Brett. "Crafting, are we?"

Brett smiled our private smile. "Stuffed animals, for the Sunset Park carnival."

The carnival is at the end of every summer. It's in the parking lot of the basilica, this church that's the size of a spaceship.

"Stuffed animals?" I said. "What, like to sell?"

"Yup," said Brett. "She's going to single-handedly save the life of Alma Lingonberry."

"Who?" I asked.

"That sick girl," said Brett. "From the flyers."

"I don't know any sick girl," I said, "but I do know your mother has a lot of time on her hands. We should make her an online dating profile. 'Sassy lassie lookin' for love. Must like salami soup.'"

Brett nudged me. "You're feisty today."

"What's 'feisty'?" I asked.

"Exuberant," said Brett, "with a touch of evil."

"You flatter me," I said. "Let's stop at the bodega."

A cat lives in our corner store, and that cat is wacko. Some days it's smacking packages of toilet paper down the aisles or knocking bags of yucca chips into the fan, and the owner is so busy yelling at it in a mix of Chinese and Spanish that he doesn't notice if I help myself to his merchandise.

Brett opened his Chinese philosophy book and started reading out loud. He turned onto Fifth Avenue, the opposite direction from our corner store.

"The bodega?" I said, but Brett was too busy reading to answer me. Lately Brett had been carrying the philosophy book around everywhere. He was turning into one of those people who all of a sudden start going through life with a purse that has a dog in it, with its face sticking out, yapping at people. I was getting tired of looking at that book's face.

I found a half-eaten chicken wing to kick down the sidewalk. Guys and girls hung out in groups, yelling and laughing and typing on their phones. Buses and cars swooshed by. People came and went from diners and supermarkets. We passed the windows with the quinceañera dresses, which are like miniature here-comes-the-bride dresses for kids. We passed places that make copies for ten cents apiece and dollar stores with brooms in every color and strings of plastic roses dangling in their doorways. Sometimes junk skipped along with us for a few steps, such as deflated balloons with curled ribbons dragging behind them like tails; oily papers from hot dogs, tacos, and nuts; broken bottles. Now and then we passed a stringy sock or a stranded shoe or pieces from a smashed phone.

We went up the hill to the top of the park. You can see the whole Manhattan skyline from the top of Sunset Park, the view people think about from postcards. It's never crowded, seeing as how this part of Brooklyn is too far out for most tourists. Most New York City people don't even know about this spot. I'm not one to go on about "Oh, what a lovely view!" But it's something to look at.

We sat on our bench. I observed that the people in the park all looked insane, from the lady wearing zigzags with the lipstick on her teeth to the oval-headed guy with the duct-taped eyeglasses. I mean, it was insane day, apparently. But it's impossible to share your observations about life with somebody who's reading a book—unless you're the one who wrote it, which I wasn't. Brett kept reading out loud.

eace: to accept what must be, to know what
___s. In that knowledge is wisdom. Without it, ruin,
disorder,'" he said.

I slumped. "Gotta hand it to my ancestors."

"Right?" said Brett, shaking his head like that was the most awesome thing he'd ever heard.

I felt like I was back at Grandpa Si's funeral. Dad and Skippy Chin yammering Chinese philosophy while red light from the stained-glass window spilled on the floor like a nightmare, and I counted the neck hairs of the guy in front of me. Counting neck hairs was the only thing that made sense with Grandpa gone. But the long-winded part of the ceremony was the part that had stuck with Brett, who'd been sitting next to me. And Brett cannot let things go.

I felt in my pocket for this photograph I'd been carrying around since the funeral. It's Dad when he was a kid in a group of gangsters with spiked hair. The one with the biggest gun is Grandpa Si. They're in a dark room, but their faces are bright from the flash. They were visiting Fuzhou, the city in China where Grandpa was born. The picture used to be on the wall above my bed, but since Grandpa died, I couldn't sleep under it anymore. Brett always had something smart to say about something, like how I always had something funny to say about something, so I knew he'd know what to make of the situation. But whenever I was about to bring it up, he interrupted me with another brilliant line from his book.

After about forty-seven hours of story time, the sun was so bright it looked like it was trying to scream. I stood and dusted bench dirt off the back of my white T-shirt and the butt of my black jeans. "It's getting boring—I mean, late." I fake yawned. Then, for some reason, I fake sneezed.

Brett squinted at me. "If my father had read books like this, maybe he wouldn't have gone to jail."

"You're right," I said. "His brain would've short-circuited. Your father couldn't have robbed a rat drowning in a puddle on the subway tracks, let alone a jewelry store in midtown."

"Very funny, Claude," said Brett.

Then there were just sounds. Birds. Laughing kids. Tree branches, rustling. Last year, our language arts teacher said the sign of true friendship is when you can be silent together.

This was not that type of silence.

"So should we . . . ?" I said. "'Cause I'm kinda . . ."

Brett stood. "Yeah, I should check in with Ma."

We started back down the hill. After a few more minutes of silence I heard clanging and thumping. Before I could yell, "DODGE THE DEATH TRAP!" I was yanking Brett out of the way of an overstuffed shopping cart that was gaining on us from behind. I swear nobody was pushing it. We watched it pass and roll into the street.

"Anyway," said Brett, "crafting could be cool. I'm gonna use it as a meditation exercise."

"Meditation," I said. "That's what cult leaders do, right? Sit cross-legged and hum?"

Brett tugged me in the other direction so I wouldn't step in dog poop. He gave me the penguin eye. "Meditation is when you try not to think unhelpful thoughts. You try not to worry about things."

"Who's worried about things?" I said.

He shrugged. "Maybe I can teach you."

"We shut our eyes for a few hours, occasionally your mother bangs a gong? Sounds like a blast," I said.

"Right," said Brett. "I get it, Claude."

As we walked back to Sixtieth Street, there were the usual spicy smells drifting from Mexican restaurants and cars honking and buses screeching to their stops.

But other people's conversations filled the air when it should've been Brett's and mine. We were all out of stuff to say to each other.

Again.

ME & PHIL THE BARTENDER

*The big lesson in life, baby, is never
be scared of anyone or anything.*
—Frank Sinatra, musician

My whole name is Claudeline Feng LeBernardin. My mother used to say that being part French, part Chinese, I've got a certain *je ne sais quoi*, which means "I don't know what" in French and is a positive thing, apparently. Course, she hasn't said that for a while. I'm eleven years old and I've got straight black hair that goes to my shoulders, green eyes, and freckles. Phil says I look like a short ex-convict.

Phil is the bartender. I used to hang out at his old tavern in Sunset Park, the Wharfman's Shore, after school. Phil would give me a glass of pineapple juice and a bowl of peanuts, and I'd wait for Dad or Grandpa Si to pick me up. That was back when Mom thought she was gonna become a hair stylist and spent her afternoons at beauty school with scissors and cowlicks. When Phil was too busy to talk, I'd spy on his customers' conversations.

But a year ago Phil boarded up the Wharfman's Shore to take the job at Guillaume's. Guillaume's is not some dingy joint with sawdust on the floor and peanut shells in every nook and cranny like the Wharfman's Shore. It's a fancy-schmancy Manhattan restaurant, and customers never yell or get into fights there, which gives it a sophisticated touch. After Grandpa died, Phil got Mom a job as the maître d', which at normal restaurants is just called the hostess.

I was sitting on my regular stool at Guillaume's, kicking the bar, while Phil poured my pineapple juice.

"Why aren't you out disturbin' the peace with Fingerless Brett tonight?" asked Phil. "He go missin'?" Phil's face is sharp and pointy, like one of those birds that snatches a raccoon in its beak, flies it to the top of a skyscraper, and gnaws it in private. His face is extrawrinkly, and his tangled silver eyebrows make me think of frosty nests. "Don't look at me," he added. "I don't got it out for your buddy!" Phil stabbed two maraschino cherries and a black olive with a toothpick and plopped the whole kebab into my pineapple juice.

Phil had only met Brett once, when I'd snuck him into the Wharfman's Shore without his mother knowing. We'd sat in a booth eating peanuts and playing checkers, and Brett had never wanted to go back. Apparently, some kids don't wanna spend the afternoon in a pitch-black room that smells like wet dog hair when outside it's a fresh spring day with butterfly sauce. Me, I'd never given it much thought.

"Brett's got double detention," I said. Which wasn't the only reason, but I didn't feel like discussing the situation.

"Tough luck," said Phil. He stuck one of those skinny straws that's useless for sucking stuff up into my glass. I took it out and sipped from the side.

"What's double detention?" asked Rita the Producer. Rita was the only one of Guillaume's regular customers who sat at the bar instead of asking for a table. She's got short yellow hair, and wears diamonds that wink and whisper, "We're not fake." When she smiles, you can see her silver tooth, which looks very gangster to me. But Rita was more of a player than a gangster. She made television shows starring famous actors.

"Every time Brett gets a detention from a teacher during the school year, Mother Fingerless gives him another one to serve at home over the summer," I said. "It's supposed to be double the punishment, to keep him out of trouble, but the truth is, Brett doesn't mind staying home. He reads books, helps his mom, whatever."

"Why does Brett get detentions in the first place?" asked Rita.

"For completely different reasons than why I get 'em," I said.

Rita smiled with her mouth open. "Why do *you* get detentions?"

Phil counted the reasons on his fingers. "Stealin', mouthin' off, destroyin' property. I've known Claude since she was a six-pound ball of drool. She's a natural deviant. Unlike my angel niece, who'll put you to sleep with the unicorns and scratch-'n'-sniff stickers, but that's another story."

"Brett ain't into disorderly conduct," I said. "At least not just for the fun of it."

"So what's Brett into?" asked Rita.

"Fingerless Brett's problem is he cannot let things go," I said. "How do you think he lost that finger?"

Rita scrunched her nose. "Something tells me I don't want to know the answer to that."

"Take last summer," I said. "Brett decides we're gonna hold up traffic on Fifth Avenue with a banner that says SLOW DOWN. I tell him he's a lunatic, but the longer we protest, the better it gets. Who knew some adults feel perfectly okay yelling stuff like 'Outta the street, ya lowlifes!' at a couple of kids?"

"Somebody called you *lowlifes*?" said Rita.

"So inappropriate, right?" I said. "And then, this red-faced guy in a Yankees cap with a nose all round like a doorknob? Jumps out of his Ferrari and chases me with a

tennis racket all the way to Bay Ridge! Leaves his car running with the door wide open, right in the middle of the
street. Lucky for us, this Ferrari's got a bullhorn strapped
on top because it just led the Fourth of July parade. So
Brett slips into the driver's seat and makes an announce-
ment. 'ON THE COUNT OF THREE, BROOKLYN,
EVERYBODY'S GONNA SLOOOOOW DOWN!'"

Rita snickered. "Wow."

"Course, I hear about that later," I said. "Tennis-
racket guy and me are busy having a dance-off at the
falafel shop. Soon hundreds of people are dancing in the
street, blocking traffic. And everybody's yelling, 'SLOW
DOWN!' The owner of the falafel shop posts the video
online, and it goes viral in less than two hours."

"I think I saw that," said Rita.

"Everybody did," I say. "In fact, before she goes
to bed, the mayor's wife gets an e-mail. From her son.
Forwarding her the link. He helps his parents do their
jobs by keeping them up to date with the trends and
whatnot. And when the mayor's wife sees us dancing,
what does she do, Rita?"

"She forwards the link?" said Rita.

"No," I said. "Well, yeah, she forwards it to the editor of the *Daily News*. But first she *cries*. The mayor's wife
cries *buckets*. And when the mayor comes home and sees
his wife tucked in bed, surrounded by buckets of her
own tears? What's he gonna do?"

Rita leaned on her elbow and swirled the ice in her glass. "Lower the speed limit?"

I nod. "Just how Brett planned it."

"Brett's a sophisticated guy," said Rita.

"Sophisticated is Brett's thing," I said.

"So how does that get him detention?" asked Rita.

"Yeah, right, okay," I said. "Here's another one, just a short one, about detentions. Social studies with Mr. H. Mr. H.—nice guy. Tired a lot, though. One day Mr. H. yawns, and rubs his beard, and smacks his lips, and says, 'Key facts about Columbus's landmark voyage. Name one, anybody.' And Brett says, 'Why do we still have a holiday for that murderer?' Mr. H. thinks about interrupting, like he did the day before that, when Brett went off on Columbus Day, but he decides it's too much work. Instead he puts on his headphones and starts writing detention slips, bopping his head to his favorite song while Brett just keeps on talking. 'According to Columbus's own diary, the people living in America welcomed him as an honored visitor from the sea, and to say thank you, Columbus captured, enslaved, and slaughtered them.' That's when me and my girl Lala Ramirez invent a contest of who can do the shortest, loudest scream, and our pal Andy Money deals cards in the back. Kids jump in, screaming short and loud and pulling out their money, stomping on chalk."

"Why are kids pulling out money?" asked Rita.

"Exactly!" I said. "Those kids never learn. You don't play cards for cash with Money. Money always wins. That's Money's thing, Rita. Making money."

"But wait," said Rita. "Why are they stomping on chalk?"

I took a sip of my pineapple juice and shrugged. "Who knows? All I'm saying is, Fingerless Brett starts the party, I make sure it stays fun."

Rita looked over at Mom, who was leaning on her elbow at the hostess stand, wearing a slinky blue dress like one of those Bloomingdale's models that take up a whole page of the newspaper. Mom even had the same mean fashion-model stare on her face.

"You're brave, Claude," said Rita. "If I'd ever been that disruptive, my parents would've killed me."

"I'm sorry, Rita," I said. "You had an unhappy childhood?"

"That's not exactly what I meant," said Rita.

Phil leaned over the bar. "Keepin' things interesting is in Claude's blood. People talk about the gangs of New York like they're something from ancient history. These guys were regulars in my tavern in Sunset Park. When this kid's grandfathers were alive, the whole borough knew it. Plenty of guys still can't sleep at night!"

Over Phil's shoulder was the big square window where you can watch a slice of the action in the kitchen. When Chef Guillaume looked through it and spotted me, he waved. Guillaume has a tan face and wavy blond hair and boings around the restaurant like a grasshopper. He always sends me free snacks, which drives Mom bananas for some reason. My snacks came out with Rita's appetizers and a plate of the chewy bread with the fluffy butter from France. It's my favorite thing, having people to eat dinner with in this world. That's what I was thinking when I started my next story, about Grandpa Si.

"Your grandfathers are *gangsters*?" asked Rita.

"Were," I said. "That's how my parents met. I never knew Mom's dad, my Pepe Renaud, too well, on account of he didn't like kids. But the real problem is, Grandpa Si died before he could teach me how to run things."

"So who's running things now?" asked Rita. "Your father?"

"Dad?" I looked at Phil. "Everybody knows he ain't qualified."

Phil burst out laughing and pounded the bar with his fist.

"Honestly, Rita?" I went on. "My life is a disaster."

"Go home, Claude," snapped my mother, who was heading toward us. As she scooted around a waiter, I saw him do the double take people always give my mother, even people who see her all the time.

"But my food just came out!" I said.

"Whose problem is that?" said Mom.

"Easy, Sara," said Phil. "Claude's all right here."

Mom's eyes are so dark blue they're almost black, like the bottom of the ocean when you see it on television. She's got a long thin nose and long brown hair with yellow streaks, and her lipstick is electric orange-red, like coral in a reef. Anybody else would've turned inside out, my mother staring him down like that, but Phil's known her forever, so it never bothers him. Mom grabbed my wrist and yanked me off my stool.

"Hey!" I yelled.

Mom dragged me into the triangle area beside the ladies' room. "You do not sit in here all night like some barfly, Claudeline, telling perfect strangers about our family. This is a restaurant, not a hole in the wall. And you do not encourage Phil."

"What's a barfly?"

"A person whose life revolves around sharing war stories with the other lost strays."

"I'm a lost stray?" I said. "I'm here because you're here! My mother! Nobody's at home!"

Mom twisted her hair up in a knot like she was sick of it. "Don't be smart."

"I'm not doing anything wrong, Mom. Phil says I can stay as long as I want. And Chef Guillaume loves me, so he doesn't care—"

"Guillaume is in way over his head at this point."

"What's that supposed to mean?"

"Be *quiet*, Claude," said Mom. "Stop *talking* to anybody who'll sit still for five seconds."

Mom's eyes were zapping everybody. Her freckles were the only decent thing. They made her look young and fun. She tried to cover them with powder, but you could still see them up close.

"I would talk to you," I said, "if you sat still for five seconds."

Mom put her wrist on her head and closed her eyes. "Enough with the guilt trip."

I walked away.

Rita's hand was over her heart, making the pledge of allegiance. "I am so sorry, Claude."

"It ain't your fault, Rita," I said, grabbing a slice of bread to eat on my way out the door. "The management tosses me outta this joint on a regular basis."

"Before you leave, say good-bye to your mother," said Phil.

"Good-bye to your mother," I said over my shoulder.

"When I get over to Green-Wood Cemetery," said Phil, "I'll give her the message."

I didn't look back, and I didn't say good-bye to my mother. The only person I could depend on lately was Phil, but I didn't feel like sitting there all night while he acted fancy-schmancy with the customers, who wanted to be kings and queens everywhere they went, and have their chairs pulled out, and who, according to him, thought they farted French perfume.

When I opened the door to Broadway, warm air sucked me out of the air-conditioning into the guts of the city. It felt like a hug.

On a normal summer night, Grandpa would've taken me out for dinner at the noodle shop, or to the movies. And we would've spent the sweltering afternoon at the air-conditioned bakery, eating doughnuts and playing cards. Or he might've stopped by our place just to give me the perfect present, like a metal chicken with flashing lights for eyes. One way or another, I'd see Grandpa every day.

I still did. Every day, I saw Grandpa on the street. He'd appear out of nowhere in his black eyeglasses and his fancy scarf, smiling on only one side of his mouth, waving for me to *Come here, Claude, see what I got for you today.* My heartbeat would sound like a train that's getting closer, and right when I was about to yell, "Grandpa!" he'd turn into some other old man. It just seemed more likely that Grandpa was lost in the crowd than that I'd never see him again. Even though I went to his funeral, and I counted the neck hairs, and I knew.

That's why I love New York City, I thought as I skipped down the stairs to the subway to take the train back to Brooklyn. *It gives you a hug without even asking what the problem is. It's seen everything, through millions of pairs of eyes. It can usually take a pretty good guess.*

SIMON SONG JUNIOR & ALMA LINGONBERRY

You have to invent life.
—Agnès Varda, filmmaker

You know how animals have instincts? One of mine is to check inside stuff, such as purses, for other, better stuff, such as money. The first time I met Alma Lingonberry for myself, I was fishing around in Mom's blue leather purse, trying not to think about noodles.

It happened the next morning, which was Sunday. Mom was sleeping in after her late night at the restaurant. Dad was leaning against the kitchen wall, talking on his phone.

"I told you, man," said Dad, "don't question it. Don't ask questions." He messed with his silver rings as I squeezed past him to get to the refrigerator. When he looked up, I was holding the door open to show its emptiness. Dad gave me a non-wave, like he was saying *hello* and *hang on* at the same time. I gave him a non-wave back and kept standing there with the fridge door open.

My Dad's name is Simon Song, same as Grandpa. Dad is a small guy with a longish black ponytail who wears seven earrings in one ear. His rings are a snake, a skull, a diamond, a thorny thing, some plain bands, and a fish. He has straight teeth and a long scar running up his cheek to his eye. The scar is my favorite part. When I rub my finger over it, I pretend it's a miniature mountain ridge. That morning he wore the blue T-shirt with the demon on it and black jeans. He was still talking to someone about not asking questions.

"DAD!" I screamed.

"Hang on, man; my kid woke up." Dad lifted his chin. "I'm on the phone!"

I put my hands in the pockets of my red jeans and kept staring. I tried to be as serious as this statue I noticed last year on a class trip to the Metropolitan Museum of Art. I imagined my head and shoulders and black sleeveless hoodie carved from a rock. I tried to look two or three thousand years old.

Dad covered the mouthpiece thing. "Don't look at me like that. I gotta finish something up. Catch you at Skippy's?"

He went back to his conversation with whoever and bumped the wall with his fist as he walked toward the front door. Then he opened it and shut it and locked it and left.

Sunday noodles at Skippy Chin's noodle shop were a tradition for Brett and me, and usually Dad showed up at some point too. But I was afraid Brett would read the whole time or, worse, read out loud. I was considering going without him. I walked in circles around our small white kitchen table, trying to decide what to do. Every time I passed our only wall decoration, a warped calendar, I flicked it. That's when I noticed Mom's purse on the floor and went fishing.

What I pulled out was a flyer. In the top right-hand corner was a pencil drawing of a girl with big ears, a crooked face, and a long braid draped over one of her shoulders.

Untitled #3

Reaching out
Was the hardest part
Now you're safe
Inside my heart.

—Alma Lingonberry

Hey there, Sunset Parkers! How's the weather in our neighborhood? Unfortunately, I can't see much from my hospital bed. The reason I'm writing is:

I AM TRYING TO MAKE 10,000 NEW FRIENDS!

If you are lonely too, or simply have room in your life for a new friend, I hope you will consider my offer!

Your Friend,
Alma Lingonberry.
Lil.Poet123@xmail.com

FRIEND COUNT: 3

Alma Lingonberry. This was the girl Brett had mentioned, the one Mother Fingerless was making crafts for.

And she was a *scam artist*.

I had to smile. Of course Brett's old lady would fall for a sob story like this. I'd have to tell her somebody was yanking her girdle strings.

As for Mom? Somebody on the subway probably shoved the flyer in her face, and she took it just to make them go away.

The bedroom door muffled Mom's voice. "Stay out of my purse!"

"WHAT?" I yelled. "I'm not in your—"

"Leave it!"

My parents' bed creaked. I heard Mom rustling for her robe.

I grabbed my sandals and ran for the door. A bowl of spicy noodles was calling me from Eighth Avenue. "Run, Claudeline!" said the noodles. "Ruuuun!"

LALIYAH "BARBA AMARILLA" RAMIREZ

I learn a lot from all the circles I live in. Even when I'm just walking down the sidewalk, there's a lot of information.
—Cao Fei, artist

I jogged past Brett's without stopping and turned under the Brooklyn-Queens Expressway to see if my girl Lala Ramirez was around.

Certain places in New York City collect grime for a living, and the BQE is one of them. You know you're getting close when filthy scraps start clinging to your legs and exhaust fumes float up your nose and make you rub your eyes and cough. Getting to Lala's turned my nostrils black, but I missed her. She hadn't been allowed to hang out with me much this summer, ever since an incident I don't have time to get into, but which had to do with spray-painting the Dumpster behind the basilica with the perfectly true observation *I STINK*. How anybody could disagree with that was beyond me, but it all got worked out with the help of a handful of cops and the parent-teacher-community meeting Mrs. Ramirez organized. If I got to Lala's place early enough, Mrs. Ramirez would still be at church, which would be, as those church ladies say, a blessing.

From a block away I spotted Laliyah standing with her hands on her hips, facing her stoop, glittering like the princess of Brooklyn. She wore a black and purple dress with long sleeves. Matching purple extensions spilled out from her curly brown hair. I couldn't imagine putting on all those decorations on such a muggy day. Or on a non-muggy day, come to think of it.

The Ramirez boys sat on the steps. A couple are Lala's brothers, a few are cousins, and the rest are friends who hang around a lot.

"Mind your business!" snapped Lala.

Her cousin DeShawn put his hands on his hips and used a girly voice. "Yeah! Don't mess with me!"

Cutie Cat stood beside Lala, facing the boys, who were falling all over each other laughing.

DeShawn stuck out his lip to ham it up some more. "'Cause I'm tough! I'm about to mess you—"

CRACK! Laliyah whipped a jump rope on the sidewalk. *CRACK! CRACK!* Cutie Cat leaped onto the stoop. The boys went ballistic.

"Oh! Son! She's gettin' heated! Barba Amarilla!"

"Lala!" I yelled.

"'Sup, Claude!" she yelled back. "Keep laughing," she snapped at the boys. "See what happens."

The Ramirez boys did keep laughing and punching each other, except for Kelvin Ramirez, who kept repeating, "It's not that funny anymore," which would make another boy say, "Barba Amarilla!" Eventually the group got bored and broke up. A few gave me high fives and said, "'Sup, Claude," before they left.

Me and Lala snapped our fingers together and took a seat on the stoop beside some flower pots. Cutie Cat jumped in Lala's lap.

Barba Amarilla is a story that's gonna get told in the movie version of Lala's life, because it shows one of the main things about Lala, which is that she's impossible to make fun of. It starts when Jamie Ramirez brings home a picture of a snake with an oversized copy of Lala's school photo for the head. The boys scream, clutch each other, all that. Lala ignores them and keeps writing in her notebook. Whenever the snake gets pushed in front of her, she smacks it, which naturally makes the boys laugh harder. Then Kelvin sees it. Kelvin with the fish lips who always sounds like he's catching a cold.

"Barba amarilla!" says Kelvin, pointing at the snake. "That is one deadly serpent."

And DeShawn starts in with the making fun of Kelvin's voice. "Is that ba-ba-ma-ma-ra-la? I'm Kelvin and I must share useless facts!"

That's when Lala, no warning, up and scratches DeShawn's arm.

DeShawn busts out laughing, but in a few seconds his arm is blazing with red bumps. "You gave me rabies!" he yells, and the boys stop laughing at Kelvin and start laughing at DeShawn. "Get him, Barba Amarilla!" they yell.

So Lala got the nickname Barba Amarilla, and she said she was glad. "It flows" is what she told me. She claimed she signed it on those poems she filled her notebooks with, but nobody could prove it. Nobody'd ever read one.

Lala and the cat looked at me. "How's your pops?"

Grandpa Si passed away around the same time as Mr. Ramirez got killed in the army. That's when Lala and Dad had bonded. It was before the Dumpster incident, when Lala was still allowed to meet us at the noodle shop sometimes.

"Ask him yourself," I said. "Can you sneak out for noodles?"

"The peanut butter ones?!" Lala clapped. Cutie Cat yelped as she leaped out of Lala's lap.

"It's sesame," I said.

"I'll text my mother at church and tell her I'm going to Andrew's," said Lala.

"You going over to Money's house—a *boy's* house—bothers her less than you hanging out with me?"

Lala typed on her phone. "Mom talks to Ms. Ildiko

on the phone and has coffee with her. She likes Andrew's family's values. She says your family doesn't have any values, and that's the dangerous part. No offense, Claude. Mom just doesn't know your parents except what she's heard around the neighborhood. Although—we shouldn't, like, try to introduce them or nothing."

"No sweat," I said. "Dad doesn't even drink coffee."

I played with Cutie Cat for about ten minutes while Lala typed, waited, typed, waited.

I had always liked Cutie Cat, how she pushed her silver head against my hand like we were old friends. Which I guess we were. Even if I didn't have family values. Whatever that meant.

"Stupid," mumbled Lala. "Whatever! . . . What? Boy—you better . . ." Lala giggled. "Aw," she said, and giggled again.

It sounded like Mrs. Ramirez wasn't the only person Lala was texting with.

I kinda wished I had a cat. I also kinda wished I had somebody to send giggly texts with. Even before philosophy showed up, Brett had never had a phone. And Brett and me weren't like *that*, anyway.

Lala held her phone in the air and did a happy dance.

"My mother said yes!" said Lala.

At least I had my freedom.

SKIPPY CHIN'S NOODLE SHOP

A poet could write volumes about diners,
because they're so beautiful.
—David Lynch, filmmaker

A five-gallon bucket overflowing with dried mushrooms propped open the door to Skippy Chin's noodle shop. It's on Eighth Avenue, in the heart of Chinatown, between At Your Service Car Service and a kitchen store called Lucky Home. From the sidewalk I could smell spicy peppers and hear the sizzling wok. The air felt heavy, like it might rain, and like it needed to.

Lala had run ahead to paint her nails at the drugstore before lunch. Sometimes she got both hands done without getting caught; sometimes she had to visit a few stores, which resulted in a rainbow effect.

Dad hadn't noticed me standing on the sidewalk, so

SARAH LARIVIERE

I decided to stay outside and spy on him until Lala got back.

When I heard myself think the word "spy," I immediately wished Brett was with me. But I'd made my decision about taking a Sunday off from having noodles together, and, actually, I was still glad. The dance floor of my brain was packed with enough stuff to think about without philosophy jumping into the middle of it, busting moves nobody needed to see and knocking everybody around and making them trip over each other and scream, "We were here first! Get outta the way!" I'd just have to describe my observations to Brett later.

From the way Dad knocked on the long yellow counter, I could tell he was getting irritated. According to Grandpa Si, Dad's Chinese is lazy. I, on the other hand, am a natural, and will be awesome at Chinese someday. I think Mr. Chin said something like this:

"What do the Songs want now? I'm retiring soon. I can't keep track anymore. I own my house on Eleventh Avenue. My granddaughter is getting married. Young guys don't understand that when you're old like me, you do this, you do that, it's all the same bag of pretzels."

Dad undid his ponytail and ran his hand through his hair. He looked at his phone and over his shoulder. When he saw me, I stuck out my tongue.

Mr. Chin is taller than Dad, with gray hair, fluffy sideburns, and a mini beard. He always wears striped button-downs with Mets T-shirts over them and a look on his face telling you he's gonna leave this conversation in about three seconds.

After Grandpa Si died, I overheard Dad tell Mom that these elderly neighborhood dudes Grandpa did business with were going to make him lose his mind. I remember Mom's reaction, too, because I was surprised.

"Please just quit, Si," said Mom, "before it's too late."

Before long Lala was back, with nails alternating baby blue and lavender. While we waited for our noodles, Dad and Lala caught up on their bonding, and I watched the crowd on Eighth Avenue through the giant window to the street. A river of people hustled through market stalls, loading up on greens and egg-shaped cakes.

A few minutes later, Mr. Chin set three bowls of sesame noodles on the counter and winked at Lala, who fluttered her eyelashes like a doll. "You remind me of my granddaughter when she was young," said Mr. Chin in English. "She got so many proposals we lost track."

Lala gave him her fanciest smile.

Dad, Lala, and I slurped noodles as we walked across the waxy red-and-cream checkerboard floor to a corner table. A gold metallic cutout of a rabbit waved from its spot on the wallpaper, which has the pattern of rocks. Our noodles were sweet and salty, creamy and spicy and cold, just what you want on a sweaty Sunday afternoon.

Lala looked up from her bowl. "What's up, Brett?"

Dad looked toward the door and held up his fist. "Yo, Brett! I was wondering where you was at."

Brett rested his umbrella inside the door. "Hello, Mr. Song, Mr. Chin. Lala."

Mr. Chin pulled out a teapot. "Just tea today, Brett? Or noodles, too?"

Brett said, "Tea only, please."

Then Brett nodded at me.

I nodded back and looked out the window.

Great. Now I felt guilty.

"Stupid," mumbled Lala.

I looked at her. "Who's stupid?" I asked. Lala wandered toward Brett, texting. "Andrew. I'm telling him we're on our way."

"*We?*" I asked. "I thought going to Money's place was just an alibi for your mother."

"Andrew needs his friends," said Lala. "If he won't leave his house, we'll just have to come to him."

"You make it sound like something is wrong with the guy," I said. "The only reason Money won't leave his house is because he doesn't wanna be that far away from his computer screen."

When Brett snickered, I felt slightly relieved, because I'd been missing him—and slightly annoyed, because seriously? I don't come get him, so he just shows up?

Lala stopped beside the cash register and picked up a

piece of paper. "Aw! It's from that girl who's making the friends!"

Brett leaned over her shoulder. "Alma Lingonberry?"

"This kid is everywhere all of a sudden," I mumbled.

Dad shook my chair. "Where's the love, Claude?"

"She's kinda talented," said Lala. She came back to the table and handed me the flyer.

Untitled #11

Odd, no?
How precious life seems?
When you're following
Your dreams?

—Alma Lingonberry

Hey, Sunset Parkers! How's our neighborhood today? Sunny? Windy? Rainy and bleak? My window is a treat but the long walk to it is not one (I'm in the hospital). So, I'm

TRYING TO MAKE 10,000 NEW FRIENDS!

Yes, I'm doing this weird thing, *but it's working!* I can't believe all the amazing emails I'm getting.

Here's the deal. If you email me, I'll write you a poem. I'll tell you what poem # to look for so it'll be 100% confidential.

What are you waiting for? Tell me all about yourself!

:)

Love, Me.

Alma Lingonberry.

LilPoet123@xmail.com

FRIEND COUNT: 11

"A dying poet," I said. "And she wonders why she has no friends."

"Ice cold, Claude," said Lala.

"Come on, Lala," I said. *"Alma Lingonberry?* Do you honestly think somebody with that name exists? I take it back. She might be the mascot for a box of stale cookies."

"Your mouth will only get you so far in life, Claude," said Dad, cracking his knuckles. "A true gangster's got heart."

Lala and Dad fist-bumped.

I dropped the flyer. "Heart, huh? That's how you got so far in life?"

"Keep being funny," said Dad. "Someday you'll need somebody's help. Everybody will be like, 'Claudeline? She don't need me. She's got that mouth.'"

Brett was sipping his tea, squinting at the flyer.

"Let's go, y'all," said Lala. "I told Andrew—"

"We're on our way," I said. "We know."

Brett set his teacup on his saucer. "Mr. Song, the best man is like water. He benefits everyone."

Dad punched me. "Where'd you get this boy?"

"Ow," I said.

"Be careful, Mr. Song," said Brett.

"Oh yeah?" said Dad, laughing.

"Don't do anything I wouldn't do," said Brett. He took another sip of tea and went to put his dishes on the counter.

Dad stroked his chin like he was pretending to think. "Like I might lose a finger or something, right?"

I cringed. *You're a gangster with heart all right, Dad.*

"Who knows?" said Brett, looking at me. Then he looked away, like he hadn't meant to.

His feelings were definitely hurt that I'd come out for noodles without him.

Ugh.

As I watched Lala drag Brett toward the door, I wondered if everybody was right. Maybe I was heartless.

Whenever I used to wonder if something was wrong with me, like if I was good or bad or whatever as a person, I went looking for Grandpa. With him I never felt like a bad kid. Or a good kid either. To Grandpa I was just Claudeline. Now who thought of me that way?

Dad took our dishes to the counter and slipped a

pile of cash under one of the empty bowls. He redid his ponytail and looked over his shoulder. "You're still here?"

"When are you teaching me Grandpa's business?" I asked.

Dad scratched around his scar. "You don't need to worry about that, Claude."

Mr. Chin looked at me.

Dad's hand was in the air. "High five, kiddo."

The inside of the church, with the pool of red light from the stained-glass window, flashed through my head. I saw the guy with the neck hairs. I felt dizzy.

"Claude," said Dad, dropping his hand, as I walked out the door.

The rain had finally started, and it was coming down hard, like it couldn't stop even if it tried. Have you ever noticed that when colors get wet, they turn darker? The sidewalk turns a darker shade of gray, and if you're wearing red jeans, like I was, they turn reddish-brown. Shop awnings, like the one across the street for the Beauty City Hair Salon, which is normally as green as green-apple bubble gum, sag, and get dimmer, and look heavier. I took my time catching up with Lala and Brett, even though he was, as usual, the one with the umbrella.

THE MONEY FAMILY

I'm a million miles away,
And at the same time I'm right here in your picture frame.
—Jimi Hendrix, musician

Andy Money is the kind of kid who if you want to hang out with him you have to go to his house, which he hardly ever leaves, because that's where he operates his moneymaking schemes. That and because he's a mama's boy. Brett says that's a sexist thing to call somebody, but why? A girl can be a mama's boy too, can't she? Except you never hear somebody say, "What a mama's girl!" Maybe that's his point. You can insult a boy who spends all his time at home with his mother, but for a girl it's supposed to be normal. Well then, I guess it is sexist. Was there an insult for girls like me, who never hung out with their mothers anymore? Maybe "Her mother obviously stopped liking her"? Anyway, I don't mean it as an insult, calling Money a mama's boy, except I kinda do, but I don't mind going to his house—and the kid's all right too. I'd tell you his last name, but why bother? Even his own family calls him Money.

Lala unlatched the iron fence and rang the buzzer.

"What's up!" said Money's husky voice through the intercom.

The heavy front door unlocked with a click. We followed the scent of roasted garlic and chocolate cake and the sounds of a blasting baseball game and an argument between Money's dad and his uncle Sal as we took the stairs two at a time to get to the second floor.

"You never, ever—"

"I ALWAYS. I ALWAYS."

"Do you hear him, Ildiko?"

"Shh! Enough already!"

"Guests!" yelled Money as he opened the door.

Money is a curly-haired pudgy kid with a groove in his chin and a savings account with (according to Money) seven thousand bucks in it that he earned selling junk online.

"Kid with four fingers! Gimme some skin!" Uncle Sal leaned over the dining room table. Brett slapped his hand.

The Money house is like one of those antique stores where everything in it tells a story in a different language. Fabrics and rugs with clashing patterns cover the couches and windows and floors. Dusty table lamps glow everywhere, but it still feels dark. An overgrown tree in a flower pot is about to raise the roof, and I'm pretty sure the dining room table with the feet carved into lion paws prowls around when you're not looking. In the living room, a home-shopping show was on low, whispering about knife sharpeners and facial concealers.

"Laliyaaah!" squealed Ms. Ildiko, whose hair was a new color, like she'd dunked it in a bathtub of raspberry juice.

Lala went into the living room and sat beside Money's mom on the footrest of the cushy chair, which was parked one foot from the television.

"Where'd you get your nails, Ms. Ildiko?" asked Lala, in her girly voice.

I've always liked Money's mom's name, Ildiko. Money told us they have all kinds of awesome names over in Hungary. His grandfather's name is Zoltan. How tough is that?

"Andrew, baby, join me and my future daughter-in-law." Ms. Ildiko shook Lala's hands. "How's your mother, sweetheart? I'm trying to get her to come over for canasta some night."

Money followed Lala into the living room.

"Gonna need more merchandise in my online store-front if I'm gonna support a family, Ma. You wanna gimme your credit card, and I'll bulk-order some more plastic crap?"

"Don't say 'crap,' Andrew," said Lala. "That word is repulsive."

"Okay, babe," said Money, patting her on the head.

"Don't pat me on the head," snapped Lala. "It's condescending."

"You tell him, sweetie," said Ms. Ildiko.

"It's *what*?" said Money.

"Money's gettin' married!" squealed Uncle Sal.

"Outta you, Sal," yelled Ms. Ildiko, "if one more *peep* I hear—"

"And now you're gonna mock my wife?" yelled Money's dad, pointing a rolled-up piece of paper at his brother. Money Senior and Uncle Sal don't look anything alike. Uncle Sal is tall and buff with a face like somebody you think you saw on television but probably didn't. Money Senior is wider than he is tall. He has a mustache and lights cigars near a cracked-open window over the kitchen sink, and puts on his clothes in no particular order, such as that day's holiday shorts with the orange blazer and the T-shirt that said PIED PIPER PLUMBING SUPPLIES: LET IT FLOW IN SUNSET PARK. If this was what family values looked like, I wasn't exactly sold, but the Money house was always entertaining. They made those characters on reality television seem as stale as some food-truck doughnuts you accidentally left in your backpack and found a month later, hard as rocks.

Money Senior dropped the rolled-up paper on the dining room table and followed Uncle Sal into the kitchen. When it unrolled, I noticed the familiar smile of a sick girl with a crooked face. *For a dying poet,* I thought, *this girl gets around.* Besides her, Brett and me were the only ones left in the dining room. I glanced at him. He was looking at the flyer too. The grandfather clock dinged. I picked up the flyer and jiggled it. "*This* freak," I said. I was working out a rhyming joke to sound like one of Alma's poems, to break the tension, when Brett caught me off guard.

"Why didn't you come over today?" he asked.

"What?" I said. And then I panicked. "I forgot."

Brett squinted. "You forgot."

I looked at my toes, squirming in my sandals.

"Wow," said Brett. "It's like *that.*"

"C'mon, Brett," I muttered.

"No, it's on me," he said. "I should've got the message."

I looked up at him and sighed. Brett's brown eyes are so deep they feel like a place you could actually go.

"It's not *you* that's the problem," I said. "It's your pal the philosophy book."

Brett exhaled loudly, like his breath was a sentence he couldn't bother turning into words.

Then he spun around, opened the front door, and left. Just left.

The sounds of the Money house faded as I followed him out of the apartment and down the stairs.

"Wait," I said. "Wait!"

When Brett got to the bottom of the stairs, he let the heavy door to the street shut behind him with a click. Right in my face.

"Jeez!" I said. I opened the door and yelled outside, "WAIT, Brett!"

Brett turned around. The rain had stopped. He was standing in a patch of sunlight on the sidewalk, beside a puddle.

"Where are you going?" I asked.

"If the mail gets delivered to the wrong apartment on Saturday, the neighbors drop it off on Sunday. I'm going to check. After that, the library."

"Your e-mail gets delivered . . . where? The library?"

"No, my *regular* mail might get delivered to the wrong apartment, and after I check, I'm going to the library. But as a matter of fact, yes, Claude, my e-mail gets delivered to the library. Unlike you, I don't have the Internet at home."

"Why are you so mad at me?" I asked. "I mean—okay—"

"You didn't forget, Claude," said Brett.

"I know! It slipped out!"

"So we've established that you ditched me deliberately. Which begs the question: Why are *you* mad at *me*?"

Looking at Brett, all penguiny with the sun on his shoulders, I felt confused. Was I mad at him? No. No!

No, just . . . I needed a break from philosophy that morning. I really did.

Hadn't I just said that?

I felt in my pocket for my photograph of the Fuzhou crew. Maybe now was the time to talk about the Thing that lived in it, which I'd been worrying about since Grandpa died. It might sound weird, but I felt like I couldn't look directly at the Thing unless Brett was with me. Because he'd understand and help me keep it far away—far enough away that it couldn't *get* me. Otherwise, as soon as I pointed it out, it'd turn around and open wide and swallow me whole.

Then again, was I gonna tell Brett about the Thing that was worrying me about Grandpa's business while we stood on the sidewalk outside Money's house, fighting?

Mussels with French fries. That's what we needed. After dinner in Manhattan at Guillaume's we'd take the N train back to Brooklyn, with full bellies, and deal with my photograph.

"Wanna come to the restaurant?" I said. "Phil was asking about you."

"What I have to do today is important to me, Claude."

Now, that annoyed me. Whatever Brett has to do is important, right? Me? Nah. Impossible.

"Same here," I said. "Amazing, huh? I was asking if you wanted to do something together, something fun, and then maybe we could talk about something that is important to *me*. Forget it, though."

Brett smoothed his hair, which was extra curly from the rain.

"What is it?" he said. "What do you want to talk about?"

My fingertip folded the corner of my photograph.

"Not here," I said. "Not now."

Brett squinted, again, like he could see through me. Sometimes I liked how that made me feel. Like nobody in the world knew me as well as he did. Other times, such as now, it made me wish I had on a mask made of steel and kryptonite. Something that would let me keep one single secret to myself until I was ready to talk about it. Which I wasn't, which I had just said. I mean, which I was and wasn't, at the same time. But which, still, I had just said. Hadn't I? I pretended something was in my eye and turned away, rubbing it.

Finally Brett said, "I do want to hang out, Claudeline. But I'm going to be busy for the next few days."

"Doing what?" I asked.

"Stuff I need to do," said Brett.

I started to ask what was so top secret. "Like—"

"Let me finish," said Brett. "Do you want to come over on Thursday, and we can hang out and try to be normal?"

"Yes," I said, feeling around the edges of my photograph. *"Yes."*

SARA LEBERNARDIN

The sea, once it casts its spell, holds one in its net of wonder forever.

—Jacques-Yves Cousteau, oceanographer

"So the cops are in my face with the 'jumpin' the turnstiles is breakin' the law' and the 'don't make faces when I'm talkin' to you' and the yadda yadda. That's when Grandpa Si walks over and puts his arm around me. We're in Grand Central on our way to the Natural History museum. Grandpa Si doesn't say nothing to the cops, either; he doesn't smile or nothing. He just stands there looking like a movie star in his tan jacket and his fancy scarf he always wore. And the cops say, 'Sir, are you two related?' and Grandpa Si doesn't say anything. He takes my hand and we walk away."

Rita lowered her eyebrows. "The cops don't follow you?"

"They're too busy on account of the five guys who appear out of nowhere in our place," I said.

"Who are the guys?" asked Rita.

Phil cackled. "He brought his goons along to the museum? The old man was an operator, no question! Wish my niece had an influence like that. Somebody to entice her away from bakin' cupcakes and weavin' flower crowns and expectin' that to be sufficient preparation for adulthood."

"What are goons?" asked Rita. "Is that a Sunset Park thing?"

I loved it when I got Rita sucked into a story. It made me feel like everything coming out of my mouth was true. Or that if it wasn't, it should be. I had a sudden urge to show the Thing my teeth. Maybe I didn't need Brett's help. If we battled, who said I wouldn't rip the Thing to shreds? I pulled out my photograph.

"Check it out, Rita. Grandpa Si is the one with the biggest gun."

That day Rita was wearing a cream jumpsuit and a gold choker. When she put on the glasses with the chunky black frames, she looked even more swanky. Like the kind of person whose office has a waiting room the size of a hotel lobby.

"Grandpa always said I'm the best person to take over his business," I said. "Because Dad—like we told you." I gave Phil a look.

"Only place Claude's father could run a business is into the ground," said Phil.

"He never expected it'd be a girl," I said. "Remember

at the Wharfman's Shore, how Grandpa would made a big deal in front of Dad and everybody about me being the one who would take over, even though I'm a girl?"

"I always thought that had to hurt," said Phil.

"How would your father react?" said Rita.

"He'd play it off," I said. "Laugh, or else ignore him."

A group of loud, dressed-up people sat down. Phil switched into showtime mode, fancy-schmancy, greeting them in his work voice with the "Welcome, ladies and gentlemen! How may I serve you?"

Mom was heading our way, wearing silver high heels, a green outfit with a belt, and her hostess smile, which, as my math teacher used to say, Needs Improvement. It comes off like she's making fun of the idea of being polite.

"Wow, you scared me!" said Rita, trying to smile back at Mom and not quite making it. "I'm sorry; I've been meaning to properly introduce myself. Claude is so great!"

Mom nodded in my direction. "Get moving."

"Why?" I asked.

"Claude's all right sittin' here," said Phil. "She ain't disturbin' nothin'."

Mom's hostess smile mixed with a *Can I have this, please?* eye thing as she took the photo from Rita's hand and shoved it at me and went off to seat more customers.

Rita put a hand on her choker. "Your mother hates me."

I watched Mom pulling out guests' chairs. The way

she did it, you got the feeling she'd like to yank them away at the last second. Let everybody fall on the floor.

"Not you, specifically, Rita," I said.

"Lately Sara's all pickle juice, no honey," said Phil, shaking his head. "Used to be Sara could watch a guy steal cream from a newborn kitten's mouth and never even blink."

"I'm confused," said Rita. "Pickle juice is an *improvement* from aiding and abetting crimes, isn't it?"

"It is what it is," said Phil.

On my way out the door I waved at Phil. He mouthed, "Take it easy."

The city gave me the warm squeeze as I headed down Broadway, which was full of people drifting toward taxis and subways. It feels like everybody has someplace to go in New York City, including me. Even if I don't, it feels like I do. I must. I'm here, moving along like everybody else, aren't I? Add that feeling to the list of things I love about the place.

When I got on the N train, it was pretty empty. An empty train is the right place to think about stuff you don't wanna spend too long thinking about. You can quit thinking as soon as you get to your stop, and if you wanna quit early, you can get off early, and get yourself involved with figuring out where you are, and where to get a decent slice of pizza, and, if you're desperate, a movie theater to sneak into.

That night on the N train I thought about my mother. It hadn't always been like this between me and her. It was never as fun as a commercial for boxes of cereal where everybody is drinking orange juice and checking their phones to not be late for their jobs, which they wear crispy suits for. But it was better.

We used to watch television together. And eat take-out, such as dumplings or chorizo nachos. If there was nothing on television, Mom asked me to tell her a story. I'd add custom details, knowing her sense of humor. Which exists, although it's not right on the surface, like her outfits. It's someplace darker, Mom's funny bone. A pitch-black cave between her belly button and her lower back. They don't make maps that go there; you kinda have to stumble into it. For example. One night, I tell Mom this story.

MOM'S BEST BIRTHDAY EVER

At any street corner the feeling of absurdity can strike any man in the face.
—Albert Camus, philosopher

Sara LeBernardin is the luckiest lady in the tristate area. It's her birthday, and Dad gives her front-row tickets to a concert of her favorite band, which is Jimi Hendrix, who is a guitar player, who is dead, but if he wasn't. Plus an exclusive backstage pass to meet Jimi Hendrix in person.

"And you shall go to Madison Square Garden all by yourself," says Dad, "on account of the well-known fact that you love your privacy."

The concert is outrageous. The whole crowd knows it's the best night in rock-and-roll history. Afterward, people tumble into the streets crying and dumping popcorn on each other's heads.

Mom, all snazzy on account of the dress from Barneys that she has been dying for that Dad bought her, plus the blowout in her hair that she got for free for being a loyal customer, goes backstage and knocks on Jimi Hendrix's dressing room door. And what does Jimi Hendrix do?

He opens it.

"Sara, baby!" says Jimi Hendrix. "You are my inspiration for every song I ever wrote, and if you do not marry me, I'll stop with the music and become a plumber."

"Don't be desperate," says Mom, kicking her heels across the room and stretching out like a cat on his green velvet couch. "You got doughnuts in this joint?"

Meanwhile Steve Martin, who is a comedian, who is alive, who is the only person on television I've ever seen my mother lose control of herself laughing at, shows up out of nowhere wearing a costume of an arrow shooting through his head. Steve Martin dances up beside Jimi Hendrix, drops down on his knees, and massages Mom's feet.

And Mom says, "You call that a foot rub?"

And Steve Martin whispers, "I know, Sara. But baby, every joke I ever tell is because of my lifelong dream of cracking you up. Wanna be my best friend forever?"

While this is happening, a team of waiters from Corsica, which is the French island where Mom is originally from, swoops into Jimi's dressing room to drop off bowl after bowl of shellfish, especially clams.

"These are disgusting," says Mom when she takes a break from licking the bowl.

When she gets back to Brooklyn, Mom is so tickled that her face is hot pink and her eyelashes are flapping like flamingo wings.

"How was your birthday eve all by yourself out on the town, Sara, my love?" says Dad, with his arms wide open. "I do hope you enjoyed it to the maximus."

And Mom yells, "Don't you have anything better to worry about besides my night?!"

So I say, "Darling Mommy, welcometh home! Happiest birthday wishes, and bless us every one!"

And Mom yells, "Claudeline! If you don't stop talking on and on about God knows what, I'm gonna scream!"

Shooting stars slam on the brakes to peek in the windows for a glimpse of the birthday girl, and the moon scarfs down an onion bagel lightly toasted with sun-dried tomato cream cheese.

And Mom throws open the windows and chews their heads off, and her insults rain all over Sunset Park, washing garbage off the sidewalks, and the birthday girl collapses on the couch and falls asleep right in her Barneys dress, all out of insults, all happy.

"The end," I tell Mom, but she can't hear me—that's how hard she is laughing.

My mother's laugh is wet and snort-filled. She snorts, snorts, and snorts, and cries, and melts into the couch, like she's laughing not just about this story but about her whole life, like that's what's the joke and you have no idea how funny it is. And you don't.

You just have to trust my mother that her life is funny. Because sometimes she tells stories about *her* mother, who lived all by herself in Corsica. Meme Alette was the toughest lady I ever heard about. She had her own gangster-type situation going over there until the day she died.

Like once, Mom tells me this story. She's eight years old, and she's visiting her mother in Corsica for the whole summer. One day she finds a puppy sniffing around some garbage cans on the street. It's black and skinny, with a limp. So Mom takes the puppy home with her.

"He had big brown couches for eyes," says Mom, "and he couldn't talk, so I didn't have to talk to him. I named him Buster. Buster was my only friend on that island. My mother refused to buy him food—said it was a waste. So I scraped meat and potatoes off my own plate. Then, one day, I wake up? No Buster. You know what my mother tells me? 'The mutt belongs to the merchant now.' 'What are you talking about?' I ask her. 'I traded him,' she says. 'For a kilo of prunes.' Oh, I cry my heart out. And you know what my mother yells? 'They're the good prunes! From Paris!' And that's it."

And Mom laughs, and snorts, wiping tears from her eyes.

Naturally, I ask her how that story is even remotely funny.

And Mom says, "It wasn't, until she died. Now, how can I not laugh? My own mother, sucking on those vile prunes, reminding me how special they are, while, thanks to her, my only friend on that island is gone. Laughing puts nonsense in its place, Claude. You got a better method, you tell me about it."

But my favorite Corsica story is how Mom used to sneak out of Meme Alette's house in the middle of the night to stand on the edge of the Mediterranean Sea. Sometimes she fell asleep on her favorite rock. A person sleeping on a rock beside the sea could not be the same person who'd been acting like she wished I was never born.

So where did all the fun times go? That's what I was wondering as I unlocked our front door. Maybe when Grandpa Si was alive, we didn't have the perfect family with "family values" Mrs. Ramirez approved of, but at least our family existed. When Grandpa died, my family went extinct. Sure, Dad was around, but when was he gonna tell me how to wake up from this nightmare? And Mom had gone from Planet Mean, which you could visit if you wore enough armor, to Planet Meanest, where only she could survive. Not to mention that talking with Brett was all of a sudden like watching television on mute—hard to follow. Only one person had died, but I was way more alone than I used to be. Way more alone than I wanted to be. I'm kind of a people person, you know?

On my way to check the refrigerator, I picked up the big black purse Mom had left on the kitchen table and felt around for something that would make me feel better, such as money, or candy, or both. I would've settled for breath mints—I was that desperate. What I found was a fat stack of flyers, written by a dying poet.

Alma Lingonberry?

Again?

Then the front door was getting unlocked and opened.

Dad's hair was falling out of its ponytail, and his face looked exhausted. He was carrying a plastic bag. "Hey, li'l gangsta."

"Why does Mom have a bunch of flyers of that sick girl?"

The hall light put triangular shadows under Dad's cheekbones as he walked in his quick, bouncy way into the kitchen. "What are we watching tonight?"

"Television, I guess," I said. "What's up with these?"

"With what?" said Dad, looking over his shoulder.

"The Alma Lingonberry flyers," I said.

"No idea, Claude," said Dad. The plastic bag crinkled as he pulled out a box and handed it over.

A dozen steaming hot dumplings.

Spicy oily happiness. Slick chewy perfectness.

I loved that man.

Dad flipped off the hall light, went into the living room, and snatched the remote. When he hit a rerun of *Happy Days*, he flopped on our green leather couch, which made a squishy squeak like it was happy to see him.

I went into the dark living room and sat beside him. The flickering screen lit up the box of dumplings on my knees. But even dumplings weren't enough to distract me. Because finding Mom with an Alma Lingonberry flyer once—once was nothing.

But *twice*? And this time an entire stack of them?

What did Mom want with some cheesy girl who was clearly a scammer and possibly a psycho, who'd cropped up out of nowhere as lame and obvious as all the other New York City hustlers dealing weight-loss seaweed superpills and curing skin problems with lightsabers and selling secret ways you can earn twenty thousand dollars a week while you sit on your butt at home—*Ask Me How!*

I mean, was she *friends* with her?

I tried to focus on *Happy Days*.

Happy Days is this reruns show where a guy in a leather jacket hangs out in a diner. It's semi-funny, but Dad thinks it's super funny. He watched a lot of television when his mom got cancer. When she died, Dad was younger than me.

When Dad thinks something is funny, he chuckles like a kid. I ended up watching Dad watch the show more than the actual show.

There was a burst of canned laughter from *Happy Days*. And then the front door was getting unlocked again.

Mom was outlined in light. The two purple drawstring bags she kept her heels inside dangled over her shoulder. "Guillaume let me go early," she said, shutting the door and sliding the chain to make a double lock. As she kicked off the sparkly slippers from the dollar store that she wore for her commute, Mom and Dad looked at each other with their tired faces. Then Mom came over and perched on the edge of the couch and immediately started chewing her nail, which perfectly matched her lipstick.

I poked her in the arm. "Are you *friends* with that fake dying poet?"

Mom poked me back. "No poky. Didja see 'em, Si?"

"I asked you something," I said.

"Yeah," said Dad. "I'll go out later."

"What did you see?" I said. "Mom's flyers? Where are you going?"

Dad put one arm around me and one arm around Mom and turned up the volume with the remote. When the leather-jacket guy came on, Mom snorted.

I yelled, "ANYONE FEEL LIKE PRETENDING I EXIST?"

Dad kissed me on top of the head. "She's real."

Mom pinched my cheek.

"Ow!" I said.

"Sure feels real," said Mom, in a voice that had the edge of a smile in it.

I should've kept asking questions. But I just sat there, feeling my parents wrapped around me like an old blanket. A blanket I loved and had been worried was lost, forever. Mom and I put our heads on Dad's shoulders, and for the first time in a long time, and the last time for a long time, our family felt like it used to feel.

Almost.

RITA THE PRODUCER

Imagination and fiction make up more than three-quarters of our real life.
—Simone Weil, philosopher

As soon as I woke up the next morning I stumbled like a barefoot zombie in a nightgown into my parents' bedroom, all ready to get some answers from Mom about those flyers. But the bed was made, the pillows were fluffed, and both of the parents were gone.

I went back into my own room and sat at my desk.

My room is not decorated with posters of fairies or a rug with purple tassels like Lala's. It is normal and plain, which I like, because it is easy to clean. My clothes live in my red dresser and my old dolls live in the closet. They don't mind the dark, I'm pretty sure.

My curtains are red like my dresser, and my window looks out at Brett's apartment. Have I described Brett's apartment? Imagine bricks for the face, windows for the eyes, and you always wanna know what's happening inside. Leaving him alone until Thursday to do his mysterious *things he had to do* was not easy.

As I sat there, staring into Brett's apartment-eyes, I remembered a long time ago, when we were sitting on our bench making observations. And Brett said, "I've observed that when your parents say they trust you to take care of yourself, it's like they're just saying that because they don't want to do the job themselves."

And I said, "Well, I've observed that, unlike most kids, I have the freedom to go wherever I want, whenever I want, so when you think about it, who's missing out?"

Last night watching television was like the old days, when I didn't care what anybody thought about my family. But this morning, with nobody home, I was afraid Brett was right. If Mom wasn't worrying about me, who was she worrying about? Alma Lingonberry?

Well, it shouldn't take long to prove the girl didn't exist. When I did, Mom could *Snap out of it!*

I opened my laptop to search for Alma online. Immediately I found a bunch of links to become her friend, but nothing else. At least nothing I didn't know already. If you don't find much about somebody online, you're halfway to knowing that no such person has ever walked the planet. But the best way to find out how real somebody is is to look her dead in the eye.

To: Lil.Poet123@xmail.com
From: ClaudelineLeBernardin5@xmail.com

Dear Alma Lingonberry,

So. I see you're making friends in Sunset Park. Are you from here? Because I'm from here, and your face don't look too familiar.

Forget I mentioned it.

Let's be friends!

In person. I am willing to travel to your "hospital," wherever it may be. Then we can talk until our faces turn green and learn everything we ever wanted to know about each other. Please send me your address and a time to visit you as soon as possible. My schedule is flexible.

Sincerely,

Claudeline LeBernardin

I hit send and shut my laptop. Then I looked at Brett's house, felt annoyed, and shut my curtains. I threw on my black jean skirt and a red T-shirt and a pair of black socks, slid down the hallway into the living room, and nestled into the corner of the couch, with the remote.

A marathon of a show on PBS sucked me in. Every episode was the real-life story of an artist. For instance, there was a lady in China who invented a city made of floating shapes and colors, and people could go live there in their imaginations. And another lady who built spiders so huge you could walk underneath them. She was born in France and died in New York City and lived to be almost a hundred years old. These were my type of ladies, I decided. They had a front-row seat in life and took notes. If you looked them in the eye, they'd be looking right back at you.

When the marathon ended, I sat there for a few minutes, waiting for it to be Thursday. My official appointment with Brett. How stupid. What was it, a job interview?

No. Brett needed a surprise visit from his best friend, and he needed it today. It wasn't like he had that much more of a life than me.

The sky was gray clouds, and the hot air made my T-shirt stick to my skin. I threw four or five garden decorations and watched them death-spiral to the sidewalk. Then I observed the shadow of a king penguin, ducking out of sight.

Did he think I wouldn't notice?

I found a few rocks and was chucking them as hard as I could until I heard Mother Fingerless unlocking the front door and ran to the N train, which was crowded and smelled like feet.

Walking up the sidewalk toward Guillaume's, I dodged elbows and smokers, feeling humiliated.

And Mom wasted no time snuffing any hope I might've had about our family going back to normal after television night. When I walked in the door, she said, "Please don't be here," held up her hand, and walked away.

I took my stool at the bar. For the first time, I noticed that the mirrors along the dining room wall all tilted at slightly different angles. I looked unhappy from every direction.

Rita the Producer was also in a lousy mood.

Here is a thing I've observed about lousy moods. Sometimes when two people are in one, and those two people run into each other, their lousy moods block off traffic, light up a barbecue, and before you know it, the two people are somewhat enjoying themselves.

"Everybody in this city is an egomaniac," said Rita. "If dating doesn't do me in, show business will."

Rita's hair had lost some of its usual poof, but her eyes made up for it.

"You look awful," I said.

"Thanks," said Rita. "So do you."

Phil gave Rita a drink. "Actors and directors, the writers and showbiz whatnot, they're needy people. They got lotsa problems, from what I can tell."

"I don't know how long it's been since I went on a date with a man who had a sense of humor about himself," said Rita. "Everybody sucks."

"Me too," I said. "I'm sick of sucky people."

"Just remembered!" said Rita. "Not supposed to use the word 'sucks' around kids! My sister *consistently* points that out. Guess what? Don't know the rules! No boyfriend! Not a parent!"

"Parents are overrated, Rita," I said. "Stay how you are."

We both looked toward the hostess stand. Mom was winding her hair around a pen.

Rita pulled a spotless handkerchief out of her black suit jacket and dabbed around her nose, like she didn't want to risk denting her face. "Know what I'm gonna do, Claude?"

"If I was a fortune-teller, maybe . . ."

"Quit my job, take down my online dating profile, and sit in cafés all day, by *myself*, and write my screenplay," said Rita.

"A screenplay is a movie?" I asked.

"It's the script," said Rita. "Your turn. Tell me a story, Claude."

"I got nothin'," I said.

Rita elbowed me. "Make me laugh. Tell me one about you and Brett."

Brett, who'd just pretended not to see me. My heart felt like a ball that had lost its bounce. If I was a different person, I would've said something like, "I need a hug, Rita." But I was not a different person, so I said, "Brett's boring, Rita. I need a new friend who's more like me. Brett's too much of a . . ." I closed my eyes, which were starting to ache, like they didn't want to keep looking at the whole dumb world.

"Your family, then," said Rita. "Okay, so secretly?"

I put my fists on my eyes. "Secretly?"

"Secretly, Claude, I want to put your family, all those gangster characters, in my screenplay. If I ever write it. Which I won't, but still."

"Why won't you write it?" I asked.

"I can't," said Rita.

I moved my fists just far enough out of my eye sockets to give her my statue stare. Like I was two or three thousand years old.

"Rita," I said. "You're a Manhattan rich lady. You can do whatever you want."

"Money I've got. Talent? Forget it."

"Write a bad movie," I said. "Bad movies are better, sometimes. All Brett's favorite old-timey alien movies . . ." I sighed. I hadn't meant to say the word "Brett."

"Brett's favorite movies are what?" asked Rita.

"Are bad," I said. "Which is what makes them so good."

Rita sniffed. "Use your family stories to write a bad gangster movie? There's a career move."

I sighed again, louder. "Who cares? And Grandpa Si would've loved having somebody make a movie about him. My only suggestion is to leave out my mother."

"I can't write in New York anyway," said Rita. "Hollywood is where I should be. California is mellow. That's the problem with my life, Claudeline. New York."

"You can't write your screenplay in New York," I said,

"but it's your ticket to Hollywood. So how are you gonna get to Hollywood?"

"I'd never fit in with that California beach crowd, anyway." Rita sniffed. "What would I wear?"

For a big-time Manhattan player, Rita sure was scared of a lot of stuff.

I talked quietly. "Here's what you write in your screenplay, Rita. It happened a long time ago, in a whole other country, back when Dad was more *active*."

THE FUZHOU CREW

My friend, can your heart stand the shocking facts of grave robbers from outer space?
—*Plan 9 from Outer Space*, old-timey alien movie

The place is Fuzhou, China. The time is a long time ago. My dad, Simon Song Junior, is about my age, and he's on a long vacation on account of the fact that his mother died and nobody knows what to do with him.

Over here, Dad likes the same normal kid things he likes at home in Brooklyn. Stealing motorcycles. Collecting throwing stars. Getting tattoos.

One day, though, he and his Fuzhou crew—since we're speaking English, we'll call 'em Gino the Goon, Farmer Mary, and the other girl, we're gonna call her . . . Sheila. Sheila the Electrical Meltdown. Dad and his crew are sittin' on the edge of the Dumpster behind the toughest dumpling palace in town.

And they're *starving*.

Sheila the Electrical Meltdown, she's Dad's best friend. His partner in crime. And also she has an unusual personal style, for a kid. Like she's got short yellow hair and wears a treasure chest of bracelets and necklaces. She also likes books, but she takes pride in the fact of putting them away when her friends come over.

Gino the Goon is the one with the muscles. There are so many people in his family, he stopped counting at 257. They all love to drink protein shakes and argue. Gino's a master of every sport, including a special kind of swimming where you do the backstroke and judo at the same time. It is very rare.

Farmer Mary hides out in the country with her cat. Every day at the crack of dawn she and her cat jog into Fuzhou along the highway, arguing about politics and whatnot. The whole time, Farmer Mary chucks handfuls of seeds into the ditches along the highway, which will grow into cornstalks so people can eat free corn. When she gets to Fuzhou, she gambles all day and all night. Farmer Mary is a high roller in the gambling world, even though she's a kid. Her favorite outfit is a red jean skirt and a black jean jacket.

Now. This is the most twisted dumpling palace in the whole city of Fuzhou. People say the owner trains mice to work in his kitchen chopping onions. People say that when cursed fishermen pull up nets full of deformed mermaids instead of squid, they sell 'em to this place, and the owner makes 'em his kitchen slaves. Through the windows you can see mermaid shadows rolling out dumpling dough, even at three o'clock in the morning.

And the owner, well. He's psycho. He's got crossed eyes and a purple face, and he only ever whispers, or screams at the top of his lungs.

That's why Dad and his crew love hanging out on the Dumpster. They love to watch the psycho owner. Because his favorite thing to do is throw customers into the Dumpster. Because he always thinks his custom-ers are insulting him. Women, dudes, babies, grannies, teenagers—it doesn't matter. The owner kicks open the back door and runs out in his chef's apron, haulin' a customer by an arm and a leg. Then he alley-oops the guy into the trash heap. The customer is drowning in paper napkins, yellin' and screamin' he wants his money back. And Dad and his buddies laugh. It's their nightly entertainment, you might say.

Until the night they're starving. Sheila the Electrical Meltdown, she's about to have a meltdown. She's like, "Yo. I need dumplings, and if I don't get them, I'm gonna *melt down*."

Sheila, I forgot to tell you, wears a lavender jumpsuit and pink sandals.

And Dad says, "Me too."

Everybody agrees. They need dumplings. So they jump off the Dumpster and go around to the front door of the dumpling palace.

But they don't have any money.

They're gonna have to rob the joint.

While I was telling my story, Guillaume's was filling up with fancy-schmancy adults. The whole place smelled like shaving cream and new shoes. Rita scooted her stool closer to mine.

"You are Miss Tall Tale," she said.

"What's a tall tale?" I asked.

"A highly exaggerated story," said Rita.

"This is a true story," I said.

Rita used a teasing voice. "Oh yeah? Your father robbed a lot of dumpling palaces when he was a kid?"

"Dad robbed tons of places," I said. "According to Grandpa, he had more motivation back then."

Rita's voice turned less enthusiastic. "I suppose he taught you to rob people too?"

"He's not teaching me anything!" I said. "I tell ya, Rita. I don't know what's gonna happen with the business."

Rita snuck another look at Mom, who was sur-rounded by customers.

I felt the Thing's steamy breath condensing on my neck and got the shivers. "Don't worry, already," I said. "It's a whaddayacallit. Tall tale. I'm giving you material for your screenplay so you can move to Hollywood and be mellow. You wanna hear the rest of this thing or what? Phil, is it okay to stay?"

Phil handed a glass of champagne to the customer next to me. "You need another pineapple and olive," he said. "Be right back with it."

"Sorry, Claude," said Rita. "I grew up on Cape Cod. My father was a marine biologist, you know? He never robbed anybody. Go on, though. I really do want to hear."

I decided to skip some of the better details, about rival crews, poisonous darts, murderous robots, and all these other things I was going to bring in. Make it nice for Rita, so she wouldn't worry about me.

Well, they go up to the counter, Dad and his crew, with drool dripping down their chins.

Dad yells, "EVERYBODY FREEZE!"

But nobody does. Millions of people live in Fuzhou, and most of 'em are in this dumpling palace. You can't even hear him. Plus, like I say, this is the toughest joint in town. Any one of the customers, from the one-hundred-year-old granny with the beard to the fat guy with the beret, could dribble Dad outta there like a basketball.

Sheila and Farmer Mary and Gino the Goon all yell together, "FREEZE!" but nobody notices. Everybody keeps elbowing each other out of the way to grab more sauces.

It's time to insult the owner.

Gino lifts Farmer Mary onto his shoulders. Dad

grabs Mary's elbow and climbs them like a tree. Sheila crawls up the human trunk to be on top. All together, they yell:

"WE WANNA TALK TO THE OWNER ABOUT HIS LOUSY STINKING DUMPLINGS!"

The palace goes silent.

Except for the chopping. The mermaid and mouse slaves in back never take a break, no matter what.

A cloud of smoke poofs out from the kitchen. And who's in the middle, coughing his head off?

The psycho owner. His hair is white, and it sticks out in every direction on account of the lightning that has struck him many, many times. He walks toward the crew, dragging one foot behind him.

Step, drag.

Step, drag.

Step, drag.

Step, drag.

He's the exact same eye level as Dad.

He whispers, "You want to talk to *meeeee?*"

What Dad can't see is that, behind his back, the owner is carrying a cleaver big enough to chop a cabbage—or something bigger, such as a kid—in half with one swipe.

"Gimme four double orders of dumplings," says Dad. "I want lots of hot sauce. And I want them for free."

Dad and the owner peer into each other's eyes. The whole restaurant holds its breath. Slowly the owner pulls the cleaver from behind his back and raises it over his head.

The fat guy with the beret screams.

"What. Do. Good. Boys. *Saaaaaay?*" whispers the owner, with his cleaver quivering.

"Stop! This is terrifying!" said Rita.

"Just *shh,*" I said. "I'm gonna make it nice for you."

"Don't kill the kid!" said Rita.

"*Shh!*" I said. "Remind me to never go to your movie with you, Rita."

I went on.

The Goon and Farmer Mary and Sheila and Dad lean over like that leaning-over pizza tower from the posters in Italian restaurants. They lean over so far that Dad's nose touches the tip of the nose of the psycho owner. They can even smell each other's cologne. Which smells like oranges and soap. Yep: Dad and the owner wear the same cologne.

And Dad says:

"What I *said* was, four double orders of dumplings. Lots of hot sauce. I want 'em for free. And I want 'em *now.*"

The owner's crossed eyes open all the way.

He screams, "Now, *what?*"

And my father says, "Now, *Dad.*"

Grandpa Si spins around and hacks the cleaver straight through a cabbage. "Four double orders of dumplings for my son and his crew!"

And everyone in the dumpling palace can breathe again, even the guy with the beret. And they all get back to their dumplings at my grandfather's restaurant, the meanest, most delicious, most gangster joint in all of Fuzhou.

"The end," I said, and took a sip of pineapple juice.

When Rita laughed, her silver tooth flashed.

Phil slipped me an extra plate of snacks from Chef Guillaume. The restaurant felt like a party where nobody ever has to go home.

"Claudeline, I relove my life," said Rita.

I dipped a green bean in lemony sauce. It tasted like Central Park on the weekend, with the grass and the fresh air.

"So write your bad movie already," I said.

"You are such a good kid," said Rita.

There was a first. She was kinda fancy-schmancy, and somewhat hypersensitive, but she was my true friend, Rita the Producer. I hoped she'd stay a regular for a long time.

TALL TALES & TRUE STORIES

I got people in my family, I wouldn't believe 'em they told me the sky was blue.

—*Law & Order*, television show

When I got home, I kicked off my sandals and peeled off my socks. "Dad?" I called, but it was quiet. I dragged my fingers along the bumpy plaster hallway wall and around the corner into my bedroom. The smooth wood floor felt calm underneath my bare feet. I belly flopped onto my bed, which made my mattress springs bounce and squeak, and flipped on my back to stare at my ceiling, which was blank.

Funny how things work out. One day you're the only kid in a sketchy Brooklyn dive bar with no windows, the next you're the only kid in a fancy-schmancy restaurant in Manhattan.

Grandpa wasn't a regular customer at the Wharfman's

Shore—regulars sit in chairs for way longer than Grandpa ever could. But when he came in, everybody paid attention. He was the loudest person in the room, and he talked fast, like an actor in one of Brett's old-timey movies. He was the best dressed, too, with his shoes that clicked when he walked. If he got curious about somebody, he'd ask a zillion questions, whatever popped into his head. And if he got going with a story about why he was late or whatever, it was hilarious. You could never tell what was true and what he made up on the spot. "I had a ten-thousand-dollar bet with the Brooklyn borough president. He said I couldn't train a poodle to play roulette. On the news tonight, you're gonna hear that the man was on official business today, in New Jersey. I'll tell you where he was: on official business with me. Gambling in Atlantic City!"

I used to see my other grandfather, Pepe Renaud, at the Wharfman's Shore too. He had thick, hairy arms and oversized fists. Mom said a tattoo of a whaling ship covered his chest, but I had to take her word for it. Pepe Renaud never talked to me—Mom said he hated kids. She said the only thing he liked was spouting off in French from his barstool to anybody who could understand him. He blended right into the place, with its dark walls full of paintings of boats tipping into crashing waves. I remember Grandpa speaking French with him, laughing and whacking him on the back.

At Pepe's funeral Grandpa told me, "Be proud you come from people who don't wait for life's punches, Claudeline. We swing first."

Incidentally, about the gangsters after gangsters in my life. You gotta remember that for me, it's the same as if your family is heavy on the teachers, or jam-packed with dentists. Careers clump together in families, I've noticed.

And gangster families are like dentist families in other ways too. Like how you're closer to some relatives than others. Since Grandpa died, I'd been obsessed with wishing I was named Song. As if having different names put us further apart than being dead and alive. When I asked Dad why I got stuck with the French last name, he told me Mom wanted to name me after her because she couldn't wait to have somebody brand-new in her family. A whole new person, with no history, to share her name with. It still shocked me that there was a time Mom was so thrilled about me that she wanted us to have our own club.

I grabbed my toes and stretched my legs in the air, like a newborn baby who just discovered her feet. And I thought, *You know, Mom is insane.* Nobody has no history, including a newborn baby. Before you even open your mouth, people make up stories about you. Not to mention the stories you get born right into the middle of, whether you like it or not.

I looked out my window at Brett's and thought about his stories, and the people who asked about them, even when it was none of their business. Such as asking as soon as they meet him, "How did you lose that finger?" Or, "So wait, are you African American or Iraqi or from the DR or what?" Try answering "What are you?" when the obvious answer is "A human being," or "What's your dad's job?" when you've never met your dad, because he's in jail for life.

That was something I loved about Brett. He didn't mind if people asked him questions. He just didn't answer unless he felt like it.

I let go of my toes and splatted flat on my bed.

Brett.

Hmph.

I shut my curtains and decided to check my e-mail. Maybe the dying poet had written me back. She'd ask me to transfer ten thousand dollars to a bank account on an uncharted desert island, and I could show it to Mom, and we could bury this charity case forever.

And whaddayaknow:

To: ClaudelineLeBernardin5@xmail.com
From: Lil.Poet123@xmail.com

dear claudeline, so jealous of yr pretty name i am obsessed with french. bonjour!

thanx 4 writing 2 me. u know what's weird? we prolly saw

each other hundreds of times in the park and never noticed. u sure u live in s.p.?? anyways, we have much in common i can tell ;)

i only have 10 minutes per day the doctors allow me 2 write email so please 4give me if i don't write back fast. will u tell me more about yrself? i get crazy happy when people email me. which should tell u how lame my life is right now! anyways, everybody has problems, right?

xo alma

p.s. keep yr eyes open 4 Untitled #206. i'm gonna ***try*** 2 make it cool like u.

p.p.s. u really do seem cool. and funny!!

FRIEND COUNT: 206
Never underestimate the POWER of FRIENDSHIP
almalingonberry/circleoftenthousand/joinus
---sent from my phone---

I leaned back and reread the message.

Kinda disappointing she hadn't straight-up asked for my parents' credit-card numbers.

Oh well. Now that some time had passed, I honestly didn't care who Alma Lingonberry was, or what Mom had to do with her. I just didn't. I'd been staring at my closed curtains for at least two minutes before I remembered I didn't care about Brett, either.

I sighed and reread Alma's message.

everybody has problems, right?

u really do seem cool. and funny!!

Was it more fishy than it was boring, or the other way around?

Did I just say I didn't care who this girl was?

Yeah. Well, here is a thing I've observed. When something is sitting right in front of your face, it's hard not to mess around with it.

To: Lil.Poet123@xmail.com
From: ClaudelineLeBernardin5@xmail.com

Dear Alma—or whatever your name is:

Although it is nice hearing from you, possibly I did not make myself clear. I know a lot of people in Sunset Park. It would be a smart idea for you and me to speak to each other. If you know what I mean. And I think you do.

Meanwhile, please answer a few questions:

1. Which street did you live on before "the hospital"?

2. When can we meet in person?

3. What school do you go to?

Nobody in my neighborhood has time for frauds and psychos, especially me. I'm trying to make this easy on you. Confess now, we forget you ever existed. Keep posting flyers? Expect problems.

Claude

P.S. I've observed that you have a phone. Please send your number, so I can call you.

I reread Alma's message; then I reread mine.

Hers just sounded cheesy. Mine sounded kind of insane. Maybe I was overreacting?

I sighed. And sighed again.

This whole thing was ridiculous.

I hit send, set my laptop on the floor, and crawled under my covers. I'd never wanted to be some kid detective, and I still didn't. But whoever Alma Lingonberry was, she'd better start being more careful. If she kept popping up in my face, she might just end up getting looked at.

MOTHER FINGERLESS

I'm just trying to change the world, one sequin at a time.
—Lady Gaga, musician

"'The universe is sacred. You cannot improve it. If you try to change it, you will ruin it. If you try to hold it, you will lose it,'" said Brett, reading from his philosophy book.

Finally it was Thursday. I had almost not showed up. I had almost stayed home and waited for my next Alma e-mail so I could spend the day becoming the kid detective I did not want to become, but would become, anyway, out of spite, simply to show Brett that I had other stuff to do besides wait for him to have time for me again.

But I couldn't help it. I missed him. I wanted us to go back to normal.

My view was an upside-down version of us in the mirror on the back of Brett's bedroom door. Upside-down Brett in his black hoodie and shorts, pacing. The upside-down poster of the old-timey alien movie. My upside-down head with my upside-down ponytail dangling off the edge of his bed, where I was stretched out, in my green sundress, which I'd worn to make a joke about how getting together was all of a sudden such a special occasion.

But Brett hadn't noticed that I was dressed up. He'd barely noticed me walk in the room. He'd been having a conversation with his book ever since I got there.

I was waiting for him to stop talking so I could start. I'd had a nightmare that a pair of tall black boots was waiting for me outside my bedroom door. Boots reaching up to the sky, with nobody inside them. When I woke up, I knew I needed to show Brett the Thing in my photograph as soon as possible. If I didn't, it might stomp me in my sleep.

And so there I was, lying on Brett's bed, waiting for my opening, while he paced back and forth, and up and down, and in circles, and rectangles, and trapezoids, reading aloud from his book.

"A sage. That's what I'd like to be. Possibly a monk. I'm not sure of the difference. In some jails, priests talk to the convicts. Do they let monks do that too? Or sages? Like, what if a sage dropped by my father's cell to talk about the meaning of life. And then, what if he found out the sage was his son?" Brett laughed. "Wow. That would be—"

He wasn't really giving me an opening, so I decided to make my own.

"Aooouuummmm," I said.

"What?" said Brett.

"Aooouuummmm. Aooouuummmm."

"Claude, stop." Brett's desk lamp shone behind his head. He looked like an upside-down glowing cutout of himself. All shoulders and curls.

"I'm meditating," I said.

"You're making fun of me," said Brett.

"No. I just have no idea what you're talking about. And sometimes other people have things *they* need to talk about." I sat up and leaned on my elbows. "Whoa. Head rush." I scooted off the bed, straightened out my sundress, and slipped into my sandals.

I don't know what possessed me to fling open his bedroom door; maybe it was something I'd seen on television. But I did it too hard, which made me feel like a drama queen, which was embarrassing. And once the door was open, I told myself, *Now you have to go through it.* Again, possibly that was something I'd seen on television.

I clomped down the stairs, thinking, *This time Brett will wonder what is wrong with* me, *and I will leave* him *alone for a few days to stress out about it. Then, when we do talk, he'll listen, for once.* I stuck my hand in my pocket. My photograph was getting soft from all the messing with it.

"Mother Fingerless!" I yelled. "I'm starving!"

A jazzy Frank Sinatra song blasted from the record player.

Mother Fingerless yelled, "I knew it, because you never get fed, because your parents are running around. Sometime I'm going to talk to your parents, Claudeline."

"I was joking. We always got fermented soy sauce and leftover broccoli, even if it *is* a couple months old."

"A couple of *months*?" yelled Mother Fingerless. "That's it. I'm calling social services."

"Ma, I'm joking! Jokes! They're funny," I said, hopping off the last step and landing on the spotless kitchen floor.

Mother Fingerless looked down at me. "You're not funny," she said. "Sit."

I took a seat at the kitchen table underneath the dangling lamp with the multicolored shade while Mother Fingerless clanged around heating up salami soup. When it was ready, she set a bowl in front of me along with a paper napkin folded into a triangle and a big silver spoon. Then she started in with the complaining, first about my behavior, then about everything she needed to do and how hard it was without help since her sisters died, and without any men around except Brett. The bright spot was her fund-raiser. She was crafting toy animals to raise money for Alma Lingonberry. It kept everything in perspective. She was setting up a table at the Sunset Park carnival in a couple weeks, and she had a great idea, which was that I help her.

I unfolded my napkin. "Sure, I got an idea for a crafty creature. It's a skeleton of a baby eel with angel wings, writing a poem."

Mother Fingerless sank into the chair across from me and flapped open her napkin. "Every night, Claudeline, I pray for you. The day is coming when you wake up and say, 'I wanna be good.' Then we'll go to church and you'll start the right direction. You know what, Claudeline? Help me raise money for Alma. No joking. For *real*."

"What a coincidence, Mother Fingerless. I pray for you, too. To the god of salami."

"Seriously! Learn something from an honest girl, you bad kid."

When I heard Brett's heavy footsteps on the stairs I talked somewhat louder than necessary.

"A young monk once told me that if you try to change the universe, you'll ruin it for everybody. Meaning, when Annabelle Lollipops bites it, she bites it. It's called destiny."

"Claudeline!" said Mother Fingerless. "Who on this green earth says such nonsense?"

Salami chunks bobbed in my soup.

"Philosophers," I said.

I heard Brett stop. I felt him watching me, from the stairs.

I wasn't sure where I was headed with the topic of destiny, but my mouth didn't know that, so it kept going.

"See, Ma," I said, "I'm a philosopher. I think about the universe, and all that."

"What's your philosophy, I'd like to know," said Mother Fingerless, stirring her soup.

I thought about that for a split second. "My philosophy is that bad guys are the new good guys. Have you ever watched television, or movies?"

"Don't sass me, Claudeline. You know I never miss my shows."

"So you know how many bad guys are heroes. Everyone is always rooting for them. That's because there's no such thing as bad guys anymore. It's like, bad guys are secret good guys, plus about ninety-nine times more fascinating, so people should do whatever they want, as long as they're not too boring."

"Who are you kidding?" said Mother Fingerless. "Yourself?"

"C'mon, Ma. Whose soul would you save if the bad guys stopped coming around?"

"I want you to come around every day and finish your soup and gain about ten pounds. And you're gonna help me with my fund-raiser, too, okay? For Alma. This is a conversation between two hearts, and I know we're gonna get somewhere with it. I'm not scared of the devil in you."

"Thanks, Ma. I'm not scared of you, either. But I don't got time for fund-raisers. I got my own destiny to live up to."

"What destiny?" said Mother Fingerless. "Crowing around like a rooster, like your father and his friends? Being idle?"

I stirred my soup slowly. Salami chunks and green flakes bobbed in the cloudy broth.

"Or whatever," I said.

Did I mean what I was saying? Did I *know* what I was saying? I wasn't sure. The Thing was glaring at me, with its jaws wide open and about seven rows of razor-sharp teeth ready to chomp. When I got close to it, my brain waves scrambled my security system so it couldn't *get* me.

I scooped up a bite with a chunk in it and heard Brett's bedroom door shut.

LALA THE POET

Right is not right; so is not so. If right were really right it would differ so clearly from not right that there would be no need for argument. If so were really so, it would differ so clearly from not so that there would be no need for argument.
—Zhuang Tzu, philosopher

As I went up the steps to my apartment, my head was quiet, like my thoughts had gotten exhausted of each other and quit speaking. When I unlocked the front door, I heard, "Hey, kid."

"Yo, Dad," I said.

I took my time slipping out of my sandals, retying my belt, and straightening out my necklace from Grandpa, the gold chain with the heart. Normally, my outfits don't have pieces that need adjusting. When I remembered how much I'd been looking forward to seeing Brett when I'd put on this one, I sighed.

Sliding down the hall in bare feet was impossible, so I walked to the kitchen on tiptoes, like a ballerina. When I poked my head in the doorway, I lifted my foot behind me for a dance move. Dad was sitting at the table, play-ing cards by himself. My heart dipped. The cards were Grandpa's. I fell into a seat across from him.

Dad dealt and flipped, flipped and dealt. "Look at you, Claude. Swanky. You got a date?"

I stared at him.

"Sorry. Pops aren't supposed to notice stuff like that, right? You'll always be my baby girl, that's all. You're growing up."

"DAD!"

He chuckled and flicked my hands off his cards. "How you doin', kid? Feel like I never see you any-more."

I leaned on my elbow, smooshing my cheek. *That's identical to how I feel* was what I felt like saying, even though I saw him all the time. But the Thing was outside the kitchen door, growling, and I needed a break from yelling "Sit! Stay!" So instead of saying "Me too, Dad. What's the deal with our family?" I said, "Is Mom friends with the psycho poet?"

Dad flipped, dealt. "Who?"

"Alma Lingonberry," I said. "The girl on the flyers, who is supposedly sick. Remember, Mom had a bunch of them the other day?"

"I don't know what you're talking about," said Dad.

"Um, liar? We had a whole conversation about her at Skippy Chin's? You said I was mean and cold-hearted, plus I got a big mouth? Nobody's gonna help me when I need it and whatnot?"

Dad stood. He was wearing his leather vest and the red T-shirt with the skull with the flaming eyes. "Want some popcorn?"

"We have *popcorn*?" I made an event of stretching my neck like a periscope to inspect our bare kitchen.

From the darkest corner of a cabinet Dad pulled out a bag of popcorn. He read the back of the bag, unwrapped it, and stuck it in the microwave.

"Whatever," I said. "I don't care about that girl, or why Mom is in love with her."

Dad sat back down. His chair scooted forward in tiny jumps, *eek, eek, eek*. Then he flipped, dealt, dealt, flipped.

I pulled the elastic out of my ponytail and shook my hair. It smelled like flowers and honey from having gotten washed that morning. I could also smell the chemical-buttery scent of the popcorn. Kind of interesting, having food getting made in the kitchen. Not quite the same scene as the restaurant, but not terrible. I shot the hair elastic at the warped calendar.

"What do they call girls your age?" said Dad. "Tweens? Pretty soon I'll be working overtime, keeping those romantic type of thugs away from you."

"Stop," I said.

When Dad smiled, his scar jumped. He took one

card and used it to scoop up the rest of them in a smooth motion, the same way Grandpa had taught me. That motion turned into a wave of sadness so strong it almost wiped me out. Except for the scar, Dad was still the cute boy in my photograph.

That's when the Thing buzzed into my ear and stung me. *Your father knows me, too, Claudeline,* it hissed. *I've haunted him for his entire life.*

My face felt hot, like I was swelling up. It was true, wasn't it? The Thing had bullied Dad, and now it had locked its yellow eyeballs on me.

What did it want from us? I mean, seriously.

"When are you gonna teach me Grandpa's business?" I asked.

"I told you not to worry about that, Claude," said Dad.

"Have you ever thought," I said, "that if you answered my questions about the stuff I'm worried about, I might be less worried about it?"

Dad's silver rings glinted under the kitchen light as he shuffled the cards to make a waterfall. The way he leaned back in his chair slightly, with his mouth twisted, gave off a funny impression. Like he was listening and not listening, comfortable and uncomfortable, at the same time.

"Here's my offer, Simon," I said. "Either you teach me Grandpa's business, or you bring me around the neighborhood so I can learn for myself. If it's like television, or the underworld from the Greek gods, and everybody is backstabbing, and falling in love, and getting eaten alive by Hydras—"

"Hydras?" said Dad.

"If you don't tell me, I'm gonna figure it out using my own methods."

Obviously, I knew Grandpa didn't live in an ancient myth, or a television show, where the worst guys have the best lines and they cut out all the boring parts. It just made the Thing feel less powerful. Like it was just one more character in Grandpa's story. A story I was starting to realize I didn't understand at all.

Dad kept shuffling waterfalls, saying nothing. He could tell me the rest of Grandpa's story, and I knew it.

But he never would. And somehow I knew that, too.

I went outside for some fresh air. A steady stream of people trickled home from work. Misty rain came in sideways swirls, like it was in no hurry to get to the ground, or to the bottom of anything, at all.

I sat on the damp curb, crunching a handful of dissolving popcorn. The mysteries were piling up. What was Grandpa's story? What did the Thing have to do with it? Who was Alma Lingonberry? What did Mom want with her? And why was Dad all of a sudden pretending to have no idea what I was talking about?

But did I feel like going around the neighborhood with a giant magnifying glass like some kid detective, sniffing for clues?

No. I wanted to hang out and do nothing.

With somebody, though.

The worst Mrs. Ramirez could say if I asked to hang out with Lala was forget about it. I mean, she could say worse, but I'd heard all that before.

Lala's phone voice is higher than her in-person voice. "I can only talk for a second," she said. "It's my turn to help with the laundry."

I scuffed my sandal on the street. "Tell your mom I'll do your laundry for a whole year if I can come over. Tell her I wanna be a positive member of the community. Tell her if she says no, I'm gonna get in more and more trouble until my life is nothing more than a horrible warning."

And that is how it happened that Mrs. Ramirez let Lala invite me over on a trial basis, on one condition: I had to chip in at the Sunset Park carnival. Mrs. Ramirez was the president of the organizing committee.

We were all kneeling on the purple carpet in Lala's bedroom next to a basket of clean clothes. Mrs. Ramirez looks like Lala, but with silver-framed glasses, straighter hair, and calmer outfits. She stopped folding pillowcases to nuzzle with Cutie Cat. "The carnival is insurance for keeping our homes safe. Everybody communicates, you know, when you pull the neighborhood together like this. And it's fun. What would you like to contribute, ladies?"

Lala carried a stack of white T-shirts to the pile near her door. Cutie Cat followed her. "I might write a poem. For the posters and stuff."

"People would love to read a poem by you!" said Mrs. Ramirez. "Will you write us a poem?"

"Nah, I was just playing. For real I can't write," said Lala.

"You can write, Laliyah. Although I agree you could write better," said Mrs. Ramirez.

Lala shook her long curls. "I hate school."

I balled up a pair of bright white sweat socks. "Me too," I said.

"Girls," said Mrs. Ramirez, "you don't have to like school. You don't even have to do amazing in school on every single thing. But if you have problems with a subject, then this fall, take advantage of the new school year for a fresh beginning. Take advantage of the resources available to you."

Lala picked up a purple-blue dress and looked in the mirror. "This dress reminds me of a peacock at the Bronx Zoo." Cutie Cat ran in circles around her feet.

"You gonna write us a poem, Barba Amarilla?" said Mrs. Ramirez. "That'd be an intriguing beginning, what you said about the peacock."

Lala talked to the mirror. "I don't have to prove I can write words on paper to be a poet. I just am one. Like a peacock who can talk. I spit it out. And so you know, Barba Amarilla is only one of my styles. She writes poison stuff, the kind of stuff that shuts brothers up. I got plenty of other styles too."

"Oh yeah?" said Mrs. Ramirez, standing and stretching. She had Lala's smile, which sometimes almost made me laugh out loud. It looked like Mrs. Ramirez was about to sneak out with a friend who was a bad influence. "Okay, girls. I've got to go to the carnival meeting. When the boys come home, tell Jamie to run to the store for pasta, and tell him it's a message from me so do so now, and tell him whole wheat pasta, please, and something green, what he wants but not lettuce. We got a chicken defrosting. There should be plenty for whoever shows up tonight. Claudeline, do you have supper plans?"

"Yup," I said. I didn't, but there was no way I was gonna sit through a lecture about taking advantage of community resources while simply trying to eat a juicy roasted chicken.

Mrs. Ramirez's voice faded as she went down the hall. "Thank you for agreeing to help at the carnival, Claudeline. I appreciate you for wanting to help other people rather than hurt them. You look lovely tonight, by the way."

One dress and the whole world's head explodes. Girls

wear dresses sometimes. Boys wear dresses sometimes. Get over it.

Lala felt my skirt. "You rock this, Claude. You should let me do your hair." I was about to ask what was wrong with my hair when Lala said, "But listen. I should be getting more famous for my poetry than that Alma girl, right?"

Alma Lingonberry. In my face, again.

"I don't know," I said, touching my hair.

Lala picked up Cutie Cat. "I was just telling Andrew how much I can't stand that girl."

"So are you and Money officially engaged?" I asked.

Lala rubbed noses with her cat. "Please. That boy thinks he's all that. He's getting on my nerves too."

I played with my sandal buckle. "You don't think Alma is some psycho trying to trick people like Brett's mom into raising money for her?"

"Alma? No way! She's definitely real," said Lala.

"How do you know?" I asked.

Lala didn't answer. She was busy reading her phone and smiling. "He says he bought me earrings."

"Lala?"

"Hmm?" said Lala, still reading.

"How do you know Alma is real?" I asked.

Lala talked while she typed on her phone. "Alma's real, all right. We should pretend to be her friend just to get our personalized poem and see how boring it is."

I was confused. "I thought you said she was talented? At the noodle shop you said—"

"Me? Nah," said Lala.

I leaned back on my elbows, sinking my arms in purple carpet fluff. So the queen of perfect hair and boyfriends and family values wasn't so perfect after all.

"You're jealous, Lala," I said. "Because Alma isn't afraid to share her poems."

Lala looked up from her phone. "Huh? No way! And why do you care about Alma, Claude? Are you friends with her or something?"

"Are you kidding?" I said. "If she's real, she's pathetic. It's embarrassing to be desperate for friends."

"If you can't make friends in real life, hello!" said Lala. "There must be a reason."

We kept cracking jokes about Alma, which should've been exactly the type of nothing I was in the mood to do. But when we said good-bye and I started walking home, the fun part of making fun of Alma Lingonberry sank like a blimp with a leak.

The dying poet was following me like a shadow. A shadow sending messages from the dark. What was it trying to tell me? And why did I have a hunch it was important?

As I walked past smudgy storefronts and fallen-over bins of trash, I found myself slipping into detective mode, hoping that the stranger would write me back.

UNTITLED #206

Trees have a secret life that is only revealed to those willing to climb them.

—Reinaldo Arenas, poet

Before I crossed under the Brooklyn-Queens Expressway, I stopped in front of the foot-massage place. I love foot-massage posters. If you've never seen one, it's a colorful map of the bottom of a foot that shows which parts connect to which organs. I like to imagine my insides filled with a rainbow of wires. A yellow wire stretching from my toes to my kidneys, a blue wire winding up my leg, tying itself in a bow around my liver.

That's when I noticed it. Next to the foot poster there was an Alma flyer.

My Alma flyer.

Untitled # 206

For a girl
Who's like a tree

Lost out at sea
I'm glad to be
Your friend.

—Alma Lingonberry

Hello, Sunset Parkers. How's the weather out there? By now, many of you know the reason I am writing to you today . . .

The more I reread my poem, the more uncomfortable I felt.

It was the part about the tree. The stranded part, and the roots all wet. Floating around, alone. The picture Alma's poem put in my head reminded me of something.

It reminded me of me.

When I got home, I ate the box of dumplings Dad had left on the kitchen table. If you gotta eat alone, I recommend dumplings. You can eat them pretty fast, so you don't have much time to think about the fact that you have nobody to talk to.

After dinner I went into my room to check my e-mail. The poem was in my inbox, too—same as the flyer. A group message. Then a bubble popped up on my screen.

LILPOET123: claudeline? yr online?

CLAUDEFENG: who is this?

LILPOET123: IT'S ALMA! o weird timing. how r u doing?!

I stared at the bubble.

LILPOET123: r u there?

Um . . . ?

LILPOET123: hello?

CLAUDEFENG: uh, nice to meet you, alma lingonberry

LILPOET123: stop! i already know u

I leaned back in my chair.

LILPOET123: sorry, that was weird, totally don't know u

CLAUDEFENG: you don't, though, right? you weren't, like, in my homeroom class? and now you got some fake name?

LILPOET123: o no. nevermind. sorry 2 bother u, claude, o, sorry sorry. bad idea

Actually, this was the most interesting thing that possibly could have happened to me tonight. The shadow speaks.

I decided to play along.

CLAUDEFENG: don't worry about it. we can chat

I took my laptop into bed and snuggled under the covers.

LILPOET123: k, great!

CLAUDEFENG: what's up?

LILPOET123: just wanted to say hi! in person, like u said. how r u?

CLAUDEFENG: not what i meant by in person

LILPOET123: i know, best i can do. i'm full of tubes and stuff

Tubes, huh? She was laying it on thick.

CLAUDEFENG: that must be tough, with the tubes

LILPOET123: it is, actually

CLAUDEFENG: so what do you do, stuck in bed all day full of tubes, alma lingonberry?

LILPOET123: just write a lot. not much else 2 do

Brett's bedroom light was on. I wondered what he was doing right now. Reading? Watching an alien movie? I sighed.

LILPOET123: r u there? did u have 2 go?

CLAUDEFENG: no, i'm here

I stuffed a pillow between my back and the wall.

CLAUDEFENG: where did you live before the hospital?

LILPOET123: ?

LILPOET123: sunset park

CLAUDEFENG: what school do you go to?

LILPOET123: charter school

CLAUDEFENG: what street do you live on?

LILPOET123: jeez. paranoid much? u should be friends w/ my mom!

CLAUDEFENG: just wondering who you are

LILPOET123: yea i get that. but like, what do u mean?

CLAUDEFENG: who ARE you?

LILPOET123: gosh, this is a fun conversation

CLAUDEFENG: just tell me what street u live on

LILPOET123: claude, i'm sorry to let you down, but my mom won't let me give that type of information. she's VERY paranoid

CLAUDEFENG: maybe she doesn't want you making friends with strangers. it's not the best thing to do

LILPOET123: thanks, b/c i totally never thought about that?

CLAUDEFENG: just saying

LILPOET123: mom reads every single email i get. and every chat, by the way

CLAUDEFENG: if she's so strict, why does she let you do this?

LILPOET123: it's called indulge the sick girl. if u r some freak believe me she'll block u. she threatens 2 make me quit but she won't. everybody's afraid i'm going 2 die

That surprised me.

CLAUDEFENG: i'm sorry

LILPOET123: it's ok. she cares. i get it

My next thought dropped out of thin air, like water from an air conditioner on the thirty-third floor, plopping on your head when you pass underneath it.

I thought about my mother. How she named me after her so she wouldn't feel alone in the world. She didn't wish I'd never been born. If I was in the hospital, she'd be a wreck.

Of course Alma's story had gotten Mom's attention.

Alma reminded her of me.

The strangeness of this situation was creeping up on me and tapping me on the shoulder. Whoever Alma was, she was right here, right now, chatting with me about death.

Unless I was imagining all this, which would mean *I* was the insane one. Which would make a shocking detective story, but I truly hoped that was not how this one was gonna turn out. I had enough problems, already.

Either way, I felt uncomfortable. The topic of dying was not something to brush off like it was nothing.

CLAUDEFENG: i'm sure your mother is scared

LILPOET123: now that i think about it, u r right, tho. u have 2 be careful, 2. lemme try 2 answer yr questions, ok? i'm 11 yrz old. i have long red hair. i luv meeting new people, writing poems, and i'm obsessed with durian ice cream

CLAUDEFENG: so gross

LILPOET123: r u CRAZY?!?! the best

Durian is a size XXL spiked fruit that smells rotten but tastes like custard. Which is something anybody could know, but it's unusual to drop it into a conversation if you don't live someplace with a good Asian market. I like it, but not in ice cream. In ice cream I think it tastes like fake bananas.

I wasn't sure what to say, but something told me we should keep chatting.

CLAUDEFENG: i read my poem

LILPOET123: o, no. hope it was ok? some r stinkers

CLAUDEFENG: kinda freaked me out actually

LILPOET123: o

LILPOET123: that bad?

CLAUDEFENG: not bad, exactly. how do you write a poem?

LILPOET123: they come 2 me, i guess? especially when i'm lonely. which i have been lately. big shock right? girl advertising for friends off the street is lonely

That made me smile.

LILPOET123: like i said tho, some of my poems r bad, i think. so so so sorry didn't mean 2 offend u?

CLAUDEFENG: i'm not offended. i don't read poems usually. it's probably good, i would not know

LILPOET123: thx!

CLAUDEFENG: so like is that why you're doing this? you want new people to write poems for?

LILPOET123: new friends. there r tons of nice people out there i might never get 2 meet any other way. i know it's silly, but i won't be around 4ever, so who cares? maybe somebody out there needs a new friend as much as me

The bubble was silent for a minute.

CLAUDEFENG: hello?

LILPOET123: your turn

CLAUDEFENG: oh. ok.

Brett's bedroom light turned off.

LILPOET123: o claude sorry sorry sorry. my doctor just came in can we continue over email?? promise 2 write back 2 all yr paranoid questions, u r a funny kid haha :P just promise u will tell me more about yrself and i will 2 ok??

CLAUDEFENG: sure

LILPOET123: don't worry claude. seems like u r having some hard times??? but u will get thru it. k??? make a wish upon the wind u never know who might catch it and send it back!! talk soon

A wish upon the wind?

I shut my laptop and stared at my wall, at the blank spot where my photograph of the Fuzhou crew used to hang, and imagined the pencil drawing on the flyers coming to life. Alma, hanging around the neighborhood. She was pale, even when she wasn't sick. She walked like a duck and wore polka dots. Overalls, like a younger kid. Maybe I'd seen a girl like that, and forgotten. It wasn't impossible.

I sighed. Time for a nightgown and some dreams. Hopefully ones without the Thing in them.

As I brushed my teeth, the bathroom tile felt cool under my bare feet. Our chat had proven one thing, anyway. If she wasn't a real person, Alma Lingonberry was a frighteningly good imitation.

I woke up to the sound of stomping across my bedroom floor.

My desk lamp threw a sideways blast of light on Mom, who was wearing her silky robe over a skirt, like she'd been in the middle of getting undressed. Half of the blond streaks in her hair looked white in the light. The other half of her was lost in total darkness. "Gimme back my stuff. Don't make me count to ten, Claudeline."

My bed squeaked as I sat up. "Give you back what?"

"Who do you think you are?"

"I was asleep!" I said.

My desk drawers groaned as she opened them and slammed them shut. She looked under my bed. I tried to remember what I'd taken recently. Was she this mad about some breath mints? Maybe five or ten bucks, here and there . . .

She whipped around and grabbed my computer.

"That's mine!" I yelled.

Mom's voice was low, like she was making a threat. "*I* earn the money in this house. Therefore, like the contents of my purse, it is *mine*."

Mom left the room. With my laptop.

I tumbled out of my sheets and ran into the hallway

to catch up with her. "That's from Grandpa, though! Give it back!"

"You're gonna end up in juvenile jail, Claude. See how you like that."

"I'm in jail all of a sudden? For taking something from your purse even though you're not gonna tell me what it was? There hasn't even been anything decent in there lately!"

Headlights from a passing car swooped a spotlight across some Alma flyers stacked on the table in the dark kitchen. I grabbed the one on top.

"Maybe I should get sick!" I yelled. "Then you'd be interested in me for a change!"

Something flickered through Mom's eyes. "You think because I don't want you stealing, I'm not interested in you?"

"No. Because you're more interested in her than me! You never want me around anymore!" I yelled.

"I am exhausted, Claudeline," said Mom. "Wiped out."

She rewrapped her robe and disappeared down the dark hallway with my computer under her arm.

"Excuse me, my laptop?" I yelled.

No answer. I followed her to her bedroom. She shut the door in my face.

"MY LAPTOP!" I yelled.

"When you stop stealing, you can have privileges."

I pounded on the door, yelling for as long as I had

the energy. My yells bounced off the walls and landed right back inside my own head. When I could not hold it in anymore, I cried. The crying was so glad to be set free, it turned into bawling. The more I bawled, the younger I felt, like I was aging backward and becoming a baby again.

But what was I bawling about? It kept shape-shifting. Losing my laptop, Mom locking me out, the fact that she thought I was gonna end up in *jail* . . .

Then I snorted. Mom wasn't friends with Alma because she reminded her of me. How stupid was I to think that? She was friends with Alma because she wished Alma *was* me. She wished I was someone completely different! Some corny kid who wore polka dots and wished on the wind.

Now my nose was running, sliming my bare shoulder, turning it shiny and gross.

All I wanted was Grandpa.

I curled up on the floor and cried myself to sleep. When I woke up, it was pitch-black, and I was freezing. It had been an hour, at least. My neck had a crick in it from pressing against Mom's door. When I stood, I almost cried one more time, just because of the fact that she never opened it.

SKIPPY CHIN'S MISSING CHAPTERS

In the depths of man,
unruly water.
—Miguel Hernández, poet

The next morning, the sun was rising behind a wall of blue clouds. The only people outside besides me were elderly dog walkers. My neck was sore, but I felt extra awake. Like I was on the movie set of my own life, but nobody had said "Action!" yet, so anything was possible.

In other words, I felt better.

Was I a morning person now? Was that what this feeling meant? I didn't think I wanted to be a morning person. They were perky and always pouring you more coffee, right?

It was probably the crying. A long cry is like a thunder-shower. The hard stuff inside you gets pummeled until it's raw, and the soft stuff gets muddy, and plants sprout from seeds you never knew were there. When your eyes dry, you've got flowers growing out of your cracks. It makes no sense that misery grows buttercups, but there it is.

Obviously, I hadn't been able to e-mail Alma any more questions on account of my laptop getting stolen by my own mother, but that was fine. I wasn't sure I wanted to write to her anymore. The dying, the poetry—it was almost *too* real.

When I put my hand in my pocket, the edges of my photograph felt mushy. And that was when I knew why I was spending my morning loitering instead of snoozing under my comforter, dreaming of chocolate chip pancakes. As I got closer to Eighth Avenue, the wind blew my hair, and I heard a voice-over in my head like they have in Brett's old-timey movies: *Detective Claude is up early this morning, off to another tough interview. Not to worry! Our girl always gets her story.*

The sign in the noodle shop said CLOSED, but Mr. Chin waved me inside. "Want some noodles, Claudeline?" He stuck a mop in a bucket.

"No thanks," I said.

Early-morning light flooded the shop. Mr. Chin dragged the splooshing bucket across the red-and-cream checkerboard floor toward the closet with the sink inside. I observed that his wristwatch had a tie-dye pattern on the band. Its neon splotches were hypnotizing.

"New watch?" I asked.

"Glows in the dark," he said.

The colorful blobs on Mr. Chin's watch strap made my thoughts swirl together. For all the time I spent in his noodle shop, I hardly knew anything about the guy. He was a Mets fan, a proud grandfather. Other than that . . .

Mr. Chin was squeezing the mop. It dribbled dirty water into the sink.

"Skippy Chin, you were Simon Song Senior's best friend," I said. "On account of that fact, I'd like to ask you a few questions."

"Best friend?" Mr. Chin burst out with a short laugh. "Yeah, right."

"What?" I said.

A bare lightbulb with a short chain dangled near the sink, but it wasn't on. Mr. Chin was looking at me like I had three noses. "Where'd you get that idea?"

"Because of . . ." I spotted a step stool and sat on it. "Everything! You talked at his funeral."

Mr. Chin shook his head back and forth quickly, like he needed to correct me as fast as possible. "That was an obligation. It's different."

Obligation, eh? I gave him my statue stare.

"Is that because you're in the *underworld*, Skippy?"

He raised his eyebrows. "Let's go back to calling me Mr. Chin."

"Mr. Chin?"

Mr. Chin took his time pouring dirty suds from the

bucket into the sink, turning the creaky faucet knobs, rinsing it out.

"Wait," I said. "Don't tell me. Clearly, I could be a rat. But was Grandpa a real gangster, like in the movies? With everybody getting dumped in the ocean and bad cops working for him and people kissing his shoelaces and everywhere he went people feeding him free pasta, except it was Chinese food? Like, all that?"

Mr. Chin rubbed his beard with the back of his hand. "You consume too much media."

"Tell me the truth," I said. "Otherwise I'm gonna think he cornered finks in the butcher shop and beat up grannies for squealing. Or maybe—"

"Cut it out, Claudeline. I don't like this kind of talk."

I felt an urge to swallow, although my mouth was dry. Once again, what I was saying out loud didn't exactly match what I was worried about. Hamming it up with the comic-book details made the Thing seem like less of a threat. Like it wasn't gonna dump *me* in the ocean, or corner *me* in the butcher shop.

"What do you mean by *obligation*?" I asked.

"Oh, maybe I'm exaggerating. Your grandfather and I weren't best friends. But Si held meetings here."

"Why here?" I asked.

Mr. Chin breathed out through his nose like he was blowing some thoughts that were floating around his brain, to see where they would go. "Because I was eager to help a powerful guy. And possibly because I felt I had no choice."

No choice? I bit my top lip with my bottom teeth and looked over my shoulder. The noodle shop's rock-patterned wallpaper was peeling at the corners. *Rip it down,* I thought. *All at once.*

I narrowed my eyes at Mr. Chin. "Were people only nice to Grandpa because they felt like they had to be?"

Mr. Chin made one last nose puff, like he was blowing the rest of his thoughts away. "Why not ask your father these types of questions, Claudeline?"

"Dad is useless," I said. "He won't tell me anything."

Mr. Chin put his hands on his hips and leaned on the sink. I could tell he was holding in a smile.

"Let me guess," I moaned. "Neither will you."

"Untrue," said Mr. Chin. "As a matter of fact, I was awaiting the right occasion. C'mere."

I followed Mr. Chin through the shiny kitchen, silent and ready for a new day of noodles, and into the stockroom, with its metal shelves stacked with boxes and books, which I quickly observed all seemed to be about improving your golf swing. We turned around a corner I didn't expect and went up three stairs with scraps of worn orange carpet on them, into a small room with a black tile floor and a giant window overlooking the restaurant.

"There's no window in the noodle shop," I said.

"The mirror behind the cash register," said Mr. Chin.

"It's one-way. So your grandfather could watch people. And look at this."

Mr. Chin unlocked a padlock on a cabinet below the one-way mirror. Inside was a ton of electronic equipment. He pointed to the corners of the room where the ceiling meets the walls. "Those speakers connect to the shop. So you can hear what's going on. There are cameras, too. If he wanted to, Si could watch meetings from my house. The video feed is rigged to Mrs. Chin's large-screen television. And this room is soundproof. I installed everything myself."

"Whoa. Does it still work?" I asked.

"Sure!" said Mr. Chin. "Lately I've been flipping on the whole caboodle when I go to golf tournaments. My son-in-law takes care of the shop, and my wife keeps an eye on him from the couch at home."

"Can I watch the videos?" I asked.

"No videos," said Mr. Chin. "Your grandfather didn't want anything recorded. It's just live streaming."

"Your son-in-law steals?" I asked.

"Not yet," said Mr. Chin. "But when he does? It'll only happen once."

Mr. Chin put his hands in his pockets and smiled. He reminded me of those old-timey pictures of men standing next to fancy cars. Like the cars are an extension of themselves, and if you want to understand them, you gotta look under the hood.

I crouched down to get a closer look. "How did you learn so much about electronics?"

"At the risk of sounding pretentious," said Mr. Chin, "a long life is full of chapters."

Grandpa would've had so much fun spying on people. I knew exactly how much fun. "This is so, so, so amazing," I said.

"Thought you'd like it. I have very few opportunities to show off. Don't get carried away, though. People got hurt, thanks to your grandfather's preoccupations."

I tried not to get carried away, but it *was* pretty cool imagining Grandpa organizing a major spy session. I felt relieved, too, seeing Mr. Chin proud. Yes, I'd just heard him say that people got hurt. Okay—wait.

I bit my lip again, as hard as I could stand it, and reminded myself that the Thing could torment me all it wanted—*I* was the one with the teeth.

I looked up at Mr. Chin. "Who got hurt?"

Mr. Chin crossed his arms. "I'm not comfortable talking about this."

I exhaled. Thank the lord of dumplings for that. I ran my fingertips along the rows of levers and curvy knobs of the surveillance equipment. Anyway, Grandpa had told me himself he didn't wait for life's punches. He swung first. And he'd gotten Mr. Chin to do all this. As my language arts teacher used to say when she assigned a stack of homework over Christmas, sometimes you need that extra push. I looked up at Mr. Chin again. "You can't tell me that watching your spy equipment in action was not the most amazing thing ever."

"Sure I can. It was a total waste." Mr. Chin motioned for me to step back, and locked up the cabinets. "Better run along now, Claude. Time for me to get cookin'."

I followed Mr. Chin back through the kitchen. *A total waste?*

He wasn't exactly making it nice for me, was he.

In the dining room we stood together, facing the mirror, which was surrounded by holiday lights. On Mr. Chin's orange T-shirt a baseball smiled. The glass mirror blurred around the edges, like it had been bolted to the wall for decades. A string of paper lanterns dangled in front of it. You'd never suspect a thing.

I didn't love how this interview was turning out, but as long as we were still standing there, I decided to risk one more question.

"What's gonna happen in your next chapter, Mr. Chin?"

Mr. Chin held his hands like they were gripping an invisible stick, wound up his arms, and took a swing that dipped low to the floor. "Hopefully, a lot of golf."

THE RAMIREZ FAMILY

Those who are unhappy have no need for anything in this world but people capable of giving them their attention.
—Simone Weil, philosopher

If you want to see something real in New York City, skip Times Square and take a long, pointless walk. That day I had a bunch of hours to kill, like usual. And once again I had no best friend to kill them with. I'd decided to make Brett wait exactly three days. Then I'd let our friendship snap back to normal, and we'd observe the Thing, and slap a leash on it, together.

Meanwhile I'd be walking alone. Walking by yourself has its advantages anyway. Advantage number one is silence. *You* being silent, not what's around you. When you are not talking or listening to a specific person, you hear everything. Engines revving. Doors opening. Music floating out of open windows. Advantage number two is that you have the freedom to move your eyes wherever they feel like going, instead of making eye contact or having to look at the ground or straight ahead so that whoever you are walking with does not think you are distracted, or insane.

That day I saw three interesting sights:

1. A bicyclist with a live cat riding on top of his helmet.

2. A school bus painted black with strands of beads in the windows and a bumper sticker that said HONK IF YOU LIKE NOISE POLLUTION.

3. Two busted pianos, facing each other, on top of a Dumpster. It looked like they were kissing. The mystery of how they got up there threatened to make me cancel all my other mysteries and investigate, and *that's* the real New York City for you—the one I love, anyway.

When the sun passed the sky's halfway point and started its slow slide down the other side, I stopped in front of a key-making shop and called Lala.

"Can I borrow your computer?" I asked. "Mine crashed."

"Hang on," said Lala.

Sunlight flickered off the wall of keys, their tiny teeth.

Suddenly Mrs. Ramirez was on the phone. "I'll sign you up for an Internet time slot, Claudeline. Please pick up a bag of green beans on your way over, as you'll be joining us for dinner. And you can tell us all how you're planning to help with the Sunset Park carnival."

Green beans!

The only thing I'd ever "shopped" for at our bodega was candy. When I spotted the green beans, I had no idea what to do. For instance, were you supposed to put them in a bag with your *bare hands*? How many beans did one person want to eat? And here's a news flash for you: *Not all green beans are the same size!* Twisted, shriveled, stubby—they're all over the place! I picked beans out of the pile one by one until I had fifty that were almost identical. Although I had never seen anyone do this, I could think of no other possible way.

I'd spent so long digging through beans, there was no chance I could leave without paying. The only cash in my pocket was the two-dollar bill Grandpa had given me for my eleventh birthday, which I didn't want to spend, but the owner didn't notice the extreme sad faces I was making as it flapped in the wind from the fan and glowed blue from the weird light of the store, in the hopes he'd feel sorry for me and give me the beans for free. He just snatched my two dollars and said, "Next time you bring the rest!" and shooed me so he could ring up the next customer.

Before we ate (fish in tomato sauce, my green beans, which I could not take my eyes off of, beets from a can, rolls), Kelvin said a prayer for Mr. Ramirez. Everybody was quiet while he mentioned how caring he was and how much they all missed him. Even DeShawn wiped a tear.

After that, Mrs. Ramirez made us go around the table telling one remarkable thing that had happened in our day, which took up the whole rest of dinner. Community activities did not even come up. Mostly people talked about stunts they'd pulled or jokes they'd told while silverware clinked against dishes and every crumb of dinner got inhaled.

For my remarkable thing, I told about the torture of buying green beans. Even Mrs. Ramirez laughed at my beans story, despite the fact that I was basically admitting I was so used to stealing that I didn't know how to shop like a normal person. Then Lala's cousin Rico put his green beans in a line and held up his plate to show that I wasn't lying about making them all the same size, and Jamie and DeShawn got into a battle, acting like their floppy cooked beans were swords.

I admit, I had a much better time than I'd thought I would. I love talking and eating with people, and eating and talking with people, no matter what. Period.

After dinner, I had to wait until my seven forty-five p.m. slot to use the computer, so me and Lala went into her room to work out a new hairstyle for me. I sat on the puffy purple mini seat facing the low dresser with the moveable mirror, and Lala stood behind me. Lala's vision was lots of tiny braids, but they kept slipping out. Of course, Lala spent half of hair-salon time texting with "Andrew," so she wasn't killing herself solving that problem.

While she texted, I examined my face. I observed

how round it is. One of the rounder faces I had seen. And the color of my eyes reminded me of a frog. Would I look older/better/less round with makeup? I wondered how I'd look with black eyeliner and purple mascara, like Lala snuck from the drugstore. Brett hated makeup, I was pretty sure.

Why was Brett in my head again? Nobody invited him.

Finally it was seven forty-five.

"Why do you need the computer so much?" asked Lala.

"No reason," I said. "Maybe I'll check the *New York Post*."

Lala's phone buzzed. "Tell me when you're done," she said, and wandered off.

I still didn't know what to make of my chat with Alma—she hadn't told me where she lived or anything. But I did know how much I'd miss wandering around pointlessly if I was stuck in a hospital bed. And that had been gnawing at me, on my walk. So I'd decided that I had to write her back. If she wasn't real, so what? But if she was . . .

After everything she'd told me, it felt wrong to leave her hanging. That's all.

To: Lil.Poet123@xmail.com
From: ClaudelineLeBernardin5@xmail.com

Dear Alma,

My computer is out of service due to my deranged mother. But try me anyway, next time you want to chat, because I have one to borrow (plus I'll get mine back, soon).

I have been thinking about when you mentioned that people are afraid you're going to die. I just wanted to tell you I am sorry you have to think about that.

Death is a hard thing to get stuck living with. My grandfather died a few months ago, and everything reminds me of him. Even stuff he had nothing to do with, such as the way the rain drips down my window, or some stranger's scarf.

And this stuff that reminds me of Grandpa, I feel like it's asking me a question. And that question is, did I ever even know him, at all? It's like he's gone, but he's here more than ever, at the same time.

I want to talk to my best friend Fingerless Brett about it, but I'm making him wait (long story). I still have my girl Lala, but she's got a boyfriend and you know how that goes.

Sometimes I feel like that tree you mentioned in Untitled #206. Lost at sea.

Do you have a best friend?

If your mother would let me bring you some durian ice cream, I would. Hopefully, somebody is.

Sincerely,

Claudeline

P.S. Feel better soon.

After I hit send, I heard thumping, shouting, and a blasting video game. It was physically impossible for the Ramirez boys to be quiet after dinner, no matter how many times Mrs. Ramirez asked them to tone it down. Lala's squeals were the whistle in the drum line.

I swiveled in the chair. What was I gonna do after this? You hear people talk about those delectable long summer days of childhood. They forget that some days are *too* long.

Mrs. Ramirez poked her head in the doorway of her bedroom. "Claudeline? Five-minute warning." She smiled at me like she'd decided I was a decent person. "You have fun with my crew here tonight?"

I nodded.

"That was some story. My sister Nina gets going like that. You remind me of her." Mrs. Ramirez was wearing a shirt with a graph-paper pattern tucked into flowy lavender pants. When she leaned her shoulder against the door frame, I saw Lala in her again. But this time it didn't seem funny. I saw how Lala might be when she grew up. Organized. With a feeling all around her that, way back when, life and her had made a deal to get along. "Of course, sometimes Nina laughs because she wants to cry."

"About what?" I asked.

"Humans," said Mrs. Ramirez. "Anyway, hope you'll

come back, Claude, and tell us some more. Maybe you can make us cry next time."

"That sounds horrible!" I said. "Why would I do that?"

As Mrs. Ramirez disappeared down the hall, I heard her repeat, "Five minutes!"

She'd forgotten to ask how I was going to help out at the Sunset Park carnival. But I'd been thinking about it, and I'd made a decision. I decided to tell her next time I came over.

For the next five minutes I inspected the framed photographs on Mrs. Ramirez's desk. This was what a regular family looked like. Cheerful. People wearing smiles so big they overflowed into their eyes. Not a single dog pile of gangsters posing with deadly weapons. What did Nina have to cry about, I wondered?

Everybody's got something, I guess.

That night, walking down Fifth Avenue, I noticed all the scam flyers, the ones that say that if you call a certain 1-800 number, you can get a car loan without a job, or that someone will pay cash for your house or turn you into a fashion model overnight. But I also noticed non-scam stuff, such as restaurant menus, ads for cleaning services, and pictures of lost pets.

There's something about a flyer. When one catches your eye, you're not clicking through Internet land.

You're walking down a certain street, in a certain mood. Paper gets wet. It tears, and dissolves.

I stuck my hands in my pockets. My photograph was folded in half. The hot air wasn't as thick as it had been earlier in the day. When the sun dropped off the scene, everything around me, the buildings and the cars, the street signs and the sidewalk, turned from orange to gray. The neighborhood felt soft and familiar, like I'd invented the place to fit me perfectly.

When I turned onto Sixtieth Street, I saw Brett on his stoop, reading.

It was getting dark—he was gonna ruin his eyes. Seeing him made me feel soft inside, like the neighborhood. I couldn't wait one more day.

"Brett!" I yelled.

The king penguin closed his book.

"BRETT!" I kept walking toward him. I waved.

He got up and looked in my direction. Then he turned and walked the other way. Fast.

The kid *was* going blind. I breathed in to yell as loud as I could.

Then I held my breath.

He wasn't going blind.

I stopped in my tracks and watched my best friend walk, almost run, down Sixtieth Street and turn right onto Fourth Avenue, to get away from me.

MILLIONS OF PEOPLE

When I lose my temper, honey, you can't find it anyplace.
—Ava Gardner, actress

The next morning, sunlight dripped off spiky leaves, splattering on my feet and the sidewalk while the wild parrots of Brooklyn cawed and flapped like there was everything in the world to be delighted about. Do you know about our wild parrots? A long time ago, a few people let their pets fly free; those pets started families; now they're just New Yorkers, like everybody else.

As I took the cap off the fat permanent marker, I felt a burst of revenge energy. I divided the first words that popped into my head over the steps going up Brett's front stoop.

YOU

ABOUT

CARES

NOBODY

CONGRATULATIONS

Then I threw the marker at his window and ran down Sixtieth Street. The squawking parrots got louder and louder, like they were chasing me off the block. When I turned right onto Fourth Avenue, I slammed smack into a man in a plaid raincoat pushing a walker. I said, "Sorry!" way too loud and kept running. I wasn't sure where I was going until I spotted the library. *Those places have the Internet!* But the sign said it wasn't open for a couple hours.

That's when the hurting started. First it stung my eyes; then it rang in my ears. My fingertips ached, and my stomach felt like it was dipped in cement. As I walked down Fourth Avenue toward Downtown Brooklyn, everything made me want to cry. Rusty gates opening for another long summer day of selling the same old junk. People standing in groups around bus stops, avoiding eye contact with each other. I was halfway to the clock tower, which is a landmark they built in the center of the action to look out over everybody, and remind us not to waste time, or something, I guess, when I felt so heavy I almost sat down in the middle of the sidewalk to wait for my life to make sense.

Instead, I turned around. By the time I got back to the library, I didn't want to cry anymore. I just felt stupid. I sat on the gritty sidewalk waiting for it to open. Sometimes people passing by noticed me and smiled, like they thought I couldn't wait to burst through the door and read every book I could get my hands on.

My heart banged its head against the wall. What was wrong with me? What was wrong with my entire family?

Concrete is not easy on your butt. I was relieved when a young-looking lady with turquoise hair and huge red eyeglasses skipped toward me with a ring of keys. She smiled like we were part of the same club. "Finally, right?" she chirped.

"Finally," I said.

"C'mon in." The lady stuck her key in a socket on the wall and said, "Let there be light!"

I didn't want to disappoint the lady, so I pretended to be thrilled, running to the shelves and pulling off books, opening them and moving my eyes around. I even collected a few lightweight ones. When enough people came in that the lady seemed busy, I sat at a computer.

When I saw Alma's name in my inbox, I felt instantly better.

To: ClaudelineLeBernardin5@xmail.com
From: Lil.Poet123@xmail.com

Dear You,

Hey. My doctor won't allow me to write personal responses for a while (honestly I feel awful) ***but please keep writing to me*** Your news and views mean THE WORLD now. More than I can say.

Love, Me.

Alma Lingonberry.

P.S. 2 those of u who have decided 2 make donations 2 help us pay our medical bills, i dunno what 2 say. except, we r humbled. as some of u know, my mother would not accept these payments at 1st. but recently, she has been unable 2 pay our rent. and so 2 u we humbly say, thanx. so i'm a long way from 10,000 friends, but this doesn't make me sad. i'm truly thankful for the friends i have. won't u spread the word?

xo almz

FRIEND COUNT: 396

Never underestimate the POWER of FRIENDSHIP

almalingonberry/circleoftenthousand/join us

---sent from my phone---

I reread the e-mail a couple of times, feeling disappointed.

But when I went back to my inbox, another one had come in.

To: ClaudelineLeBernardin5@xmail.com
From: Lil.Poet123@xmail.com

dear claudeline SHH sneaking this, sorry have 2 make it fast

thanx 4 your note and everything u said. u have a lot of

sadness in your life, girl, u don't deserve it. wish we could talk on the phone. hang in there k? tell me more b/c i'm worried about u? how do u stay strong?? maybe i can learn from u. xo alma

p.s. sorry so short. more soon promise.

p.p.s. this whole place smells like soup. i hate soup!

FRIEND COUNT: 396

Never underestimate the POWER of FRIENDSHIP

almalingonberry/circleoftenthousand/join us

---sent from my phone---

To: Lil.Poet123@xmail.com

From: ClaudelineLeBernardin5@xmail.com

Dear Alma,

Maybe you should tell your doctors about the soup? It's rude to force you to smell something gross while you are sick. Like torture.

How are you doing? I mean, what's going on with your sickness? Also, what is it that you are sick with, again? If you feel like talking about it. I know you can't write back at the moment. But I'm thinking of you.

You ask me to tell you how I stay strong, well the answer is I don't. For instance, I just did something, to try to make a point. And the point I was trying to make was, who needs you anyway? (Not you. Somebody else.) But I made a different point, by accident. Which is that my personality is a disease, and hurting people is my destiny, and it's coming for me.

That probably makes no sense. The problem is, Alma, my grandfather died because he was a gangster. My whole family is gangsters. I didn't used to think much about it.

But what if it's a curse?

Sorry for the sob story. By the way, I'm gonna help an old lady I know who is making stuff and selling it for you. I'm supposed to volunteer at the carnival anyway so it's no big deal.

Your friend,

Claude

After I left the library, I took my photograph out of my pocket and walked around trying to force myself to think about Grandpa and the Thing. *No, his personality wasn't a barrel of sugar cubes drizzled in butterscotch,* I thought . . .

But that was as far as I got. I switched to writing an imaginary e-mail to Alma in my head, describing the salt-and-pepper-haired lady who works at the post office and chews on the inside of her cheek and who always tells me to look sharp. Not that I ever go into the post office. I only see her when she's opening the gates or locking them down. "Look sharp," she says, like she's my lookout and she's been standing there chewing her cheek and keeping an eye on possible threats since the last time I passed by. I even added custom details I thought Alma would appreciate, like a street poet who collects change in a construction hat and the pet python he keeps in his duffel bag.

Laughter *was* the best medicine. Just pretending to write to Alma, making everything as funny as possible, put me in a better mood. When it started getting dark, I jogged home, coughing BQE dust and feeling relieved, like I'd discovered the secret to life. Focus on the funny parts.

When I turned onto Sixtieth Street, I saw soapy bubbles melting down Brett's steps. The words I'd written had faded, but even in the sunset they weren't completely gone. They were fingerprints from a heartless ghost.

The secret to life went, *Poof! Nice try.*

A voice inside my stomach said, *Ugh.*

SHADOWS

Death and life have their determined appointments.
—Confucius, philosopher

From the sidewalk, I saw three orange-gold rectangles lighting up our apartment. A human must've been home. Why tonight, of all nights? I was sick of humans. I let myself in and shook my feet to make my sandals fly off and hit the wall. The two humans were in the kitchen, arguing. One of them was the mama human, who must've come home from work early, saying, "They're sending money without being asked," and the other was the papa human, saying, "Let me handle it, Sara," and then the kid human shut her door, put on her nightgown, and went to bed early. The excitement I'd felt about writing to Alma had dribbled down the gutter through the metal drain in the street to wherever that goes, the sewer or maybe the sea.

All night I lay on top of my comforter with my eyes pasted open like a fish. When it felt like morning—had five seconds passed? Five years?—I threw on my red jeans and a blue T-shirt and headed back outside. From the hallway I noticed Mom, sitting at the kitchen table with her head in her hands. She wore a satiny violet pantsuit thing with black high heels. It was a little early to be dressed for work. But we hadn't talked since that argument in the middle of the night, so I decided not to ask about that, and went with a casual conversation-starter instead.

"I like your outfit," I said.

"Don't push it, Claude," muttered Mom.

I swear, I didn't know how Mom kept her hostess job. She couldn't make pleasant small talk if you paid her. And Guillaume *did* pay her—*to do exactly that*.

"Gimme back my laptop, lady, and I won't," I said.

The look Mom gave me could've turned fireworks to snow. "Stay outta trouble, and I'll consider it."

"Trouble," I mumbled as I collected my sandals and unlocked the front door. "Tell it to stay out of me."

They say a criminal always returns to the scene of the crime. I used to wonder about the reason for that. I still can't tell you what it is.

A scrub brush and a bucket of suds propped open Brett's front door to let in the breeze. You couldn't see the kitchen table underneath the ribbons, buttons, and doodads Mother Fingerless was using to craft her creatures. You almost couldn't see *her* behind the pile of furry fish, patchwork snakes, and shiny puff balls that might have been . . . chipmunks? And she ain't the daintiest dame who ever stuffed a teddy bear. The hanging lamp with the multicolored shade reminded me of a circus tent.

I took a seat. "Yo," I said.

Mother Fingerless poked her head around the pile. "Baby girl! I knew it!" She slapped the table and shoved a poofy donkey—or was it a horse?—in my face. "You want to help. Decorate this!"

"Aw, I'm gonna help you with your table at the carnival. I gotta decorate stuff too?"

"That's the spirit, baby girl! And yes, you gotta decorate stuff too. Neon, spotted, natural. However you want. Look at my sequins. I got eight colors. Where you been lately?"

Creak, trudge, creak, trudge. I heard Brett's heavy footsteps coming down the stairs. His personal soundtrack. He was holding his Chinese philosophy book and an envelope. He went into the living room and turned on the television.

Mother Fingerless wasn't paying much attention to the donkey-horse as she scribbled on it with a smelly pink marker. She whispered, "My son is in a mood today. He still thinks that guy is gonna write him back. I tell him that man has never been no help to anybody, and Brett is gonna get his heart broke. Like me. But Brett has his own ideas."

I took a stuffed turtle with a painted-on grin from the creature pile and twisted open a glue bottle. "Who's supposed to write him back?" I whispered.

"His *father*," she whispered.

I squirted glue on the turtle. "His father gets e-mail in jail?"

"Letters." Mother Fingerless made her mouth into a line, like a ruler.

"His father didn't write him back?"

Mother Fingerless shook her head.

I looked at Brett, hunched over his book, with an old-timey movie in the background. The envelope was next to him, on a splashy throw pillow.

Mother Fingerless was having a hard time attaching sequins to a bird, or a dolphin, maybe, that she'd stamped with orange stars. She stuck out her tongue. "This one is *bleh*. It was a fish, but now it looks more like a cat. Maybe somebody will love it like this." She crossed her eyes and held her throat.

I kept an eye on Brett. "It's a sea turkey."

Mother Fingerless whooped loudly. "Brett! Come help us make sea turkeys for Alma!"

"Yeah, come help us," I added quietly.

Brett turned up the volume.

My heart felt like a swamp, and I was sinking in it. The sticky turtle was still in my hand. I used it to mop up green glitter from a paper plate, and then I set it on the table, facing me. Now it was alive, twinkling and grinning. It didn't know any better.

I whispered, "If his father didn't write him back, what's in the envelope?"

Mother Fingerless calmed down her laughing. "A letter from his grandmother. His father's mother."

I felt relieved. "So somebody *did* write him back."

Mother Fingerless shook her head in an exaggerated way and spoke quietly. "The lady says as far as she's concerned, her son don't exist, and therefore Brett . . . Well, it's not a good letter, and I keep trying to throw it away, but Brett says he has to keep it. He carries it with him so I can't grab it. If you get a chance, snatch that letter, Claude. Burn it up, because that type of thing don't do nobody no favors."

I looked at Brett, sitting in the shadows with his book.

When I left Brett's, I observed that the walk between our apartments had stretched, along with our friendship. Rubber bands, bubble gum, waistbands, balloons. They stretch until they can't snap back. The distance between when we were best friends and now felt almost impossible to cross. In science we learned the word "eons." I forget exactly what it means, but it is the right word to describe this distance. And now that we were eons apart, I needed more than ever to reach him. What type of transportation crosses eons? Not feet. Not the N train. What?

Nobody was home. On my desk was my laptop. There was also a piece of stationery with a teddy bear on it and a note in Mom's handwriting.

Claudeline,
You may have your computer back now. Want to keep it?
Stop stealing.
Mom

You couldn't accuse the woman of overexplaining herself.

For once I didn't feel like checking my e-mail. Instead I stared out my window, trying to figure out what, exactly, had gone wrong between Brett and me. But as soon as I started working on that problem, I spotted the Thing outside in the shadows, chomping and sloshing its tongue around, so I opened my desk drawer and took out the thick book of word searches I'd stolen from the language arts closet. Word searches are okay, as far as language arts is concerned. Circling words makes time pass without you having to feel the ten billion things that are infecting your blood and rusting your bones. I dug out a pencil and crawled into bed. The confetti of letters blurred together, then unblurred into crystal-clear things, one by one.

SUITCASE.
COCONUT.
KOALA.

When I woke up, the word-search book was a paper sculpture on the floor, and it was dark. I didn't even remember falling asleep.

The park at night is the one place in the neighborhood Grandpa said was unsafe. He told me never to go there alone.

But what did Grandpa know about staying safe?

Nothing, obviously.

Soggy clouds soaked up the streetlights and muffed out the moon. The blob that ate Brooklyn, dark black. And there were people. Too many people drifting in too many shadows. It was the kind of night when stuff happens that nobody sees, nobody will talk about, no matter how many times you ask.

Brett wasn't gonna be with me when I looked directly at the Thing I'd been worrying about since Grandpa died.

Nobody was.

Maybe that was the only way. To stare right back at it. Alone.

The neighborhood was layered with smoky shapes. Floating black, liquid blue, gray-yellow. A cool wind swished my hair around my neck. Up ahead I saw a shadow in a long coat, and for a second it happened— my heart beat like a train rushing toward me and I knew for a *fact* it was Grandpa.

But it wasn't. Because the truth is, Grandpa got shot.

He got murdered, right here in Sunset Park. No matter how many articles I read in the newspaper—and there weren't enough; shouldn't every single article in every single newspaper be talking about this, every single second of every single day, forever? What else mattered? I'd never understood what happened, and nobody would explain it to me.

But that wasn't even what I was the most worried about.

If somebody was mad enough at Grandpa to kill him, was there another kid outside tonight, somebody just like me, with her brain waves all crisscrossed, and her heart sliced open, seeing dead people walking down crowded streets, only it was *because of Grandpa Si*?

What was Grandpa's business? Not the glamorous stuff from the movies about wearing slick suits and bribing politicians and teaming up with dirty cops. Not the myths about powerful gods and goddesses battling to the death and shaking out the pockets of the mortals who got caught in the crossfire and slaughtered on the battlefield so the gold could rain out for whoever wanted to scramble over all those dead bodies, collecting it. Not the television shows where the good guys and the bad guys bleed together until the whole world feels like a mess nobody can hold their breath long enough to clean up.

Did Grandpa hurt people?

The wind stung my eyes. As I got closer to our bench,

a glob of shadows jostled. A cracked voice yelled, "You! Kid! C'mere!"

I turned around and sprinted down the hill. When I got to the street, I was out of breath, and my hair was sticking to my mouth.

But I couldn't go home yet. Even if I admitted the rest of Grandpa's story—that the Thing that had destroyed my family destroyed other people's families too—

Because the Thing is *people hurting people*, spreading pain like it is *fun*, like it is *nothing*—

And even if I knew it wasn't just gangsters, it's everybody, posing with violence like it is our pet, some prop we can use to look tough—

Or does the Thing use us?—

I still didn't know who *I* was. Why I, Claudeline, would want to hurt Brett, my best friend, who didn't deserve it.

I forced myself to keep walking. Walking and walking through the blackness, searching for answers.

As I got closer to the Brooklyn-Queens Expressway, I heard waves of crinkling noises, like a bunch of papers flapping in the wind.

It was a fresh batch of Alma flyers. Hundreds of fluttering Alma flyers stuck with packing tape to the pillars below the highway. They were all the same, except on different-colored paper. Light pink, light green, light blue, and light yellow. Each one had a giant version of the drawing of Alma smack in the middle. Underneath, they said:

WE BELIEVE IN FRIENDSHIP
join us.
almalingonberry/circleoftenthousand/joinus
lilpoet.123@xmail.com

I would describe the mood the flyers created as a grimy Easter.

I would describe the shadow drifting under the BQE posting them as a guy with long black hair, a leather vest, rings on every finger, and an ear with seven piercings, including one of a scorpion, one of a skull, and one of the skeleton of a fish.

Big, fat, slow-motion raindrops started bursting on the ground like water balloons.

What was he doing? What was he *doing*?

What was he doing?

I ran. When I got home, I went straight to my bedroom and barricaded my door with my dresser. I leaned against it, out of breath.

What on this green earth is going on?

THE MONEYMAN

I have a certain experience of the way people tell lies.
—Miss Marple, detective from a book

My room glowed like fire from the morning light blazing through my red curtains. My blue T-shirt was twisted into a bunch under one of my armpits, and my bracelet was attached to my mouth. My clothes were still damp from the rain. I stretched out on my bed like a big letter *X*, then leaned on my elbows. My red dresser was solid, blocking my door. My faithful bodyguard.

Yes: A barricade did seem overly dramatic, now that I had gotten some sleep.

But a girl couldn't be too careful these days.

Socks. Red socks to bodyguard my bare toes. I wanted them. How handy that my sock drawer was on my way out the door. I hopped on one foot, then the other, pulling on my socks; then I used my shoulder, then both arms, then my back to shove my dresser out of the way, and crept down the hall and outside before anybody was awake.

I stood on the sidewalk, unsure what to do. Trees spilled leftover rain, sloppy splashes in the wind.

It was Sunday, but I knew Brett would not want noodles. My brain was so messy I couldn't even find a place to sit down, let alone use it to cross eons. Anyway, I had zero appetite.

I'd spent the night dreaming I was writing Dad an endless e-mail describing my vacation in Timbuktu. Now, I've never been to Timbuktu, and I could not point it out on a globe, even for ten thousand dollars. But a book about the place had caught my eye at the library. It was on top of the pile I wound up leaving next to the computer. On the cover was a desert, and writing in English, along with a language that uses calligraphy— like Chinese, but not. In my dream I told Dad I'd seen Grandpa in Timbuktu, only he was speaking this other language, while pink pterodactyls folded paper airplanes and a swarm of bees spelled the word "HELLO!" And somehow I knew I was invisible—but the details aren't the point. The point is, I was e-mailing *Dad*.

There were plenty of boring explanations for Dad posting Alma flyers. The simplest was that he was helping her. He was a gangster with heart, like he'd said that time at the noodle shop.

But if that was it, how come when I'd asked about Alma since then, he'd acted like he didn't know what I was talking about? And if Dad was posting flyers, he definitely knew why Mom had piles of them. What were they hiding from me?

Something was going on with my parents and Alma Lingonberry. Something shady, right in front of my face, begging me to open my eyes.

I sat on the curb, biting the edge of my phone. I couldn't talk to Lala about this. I didn't want to admit that I'd made friends with Alma.

Should I call *Money*?

Money is my friend the way a roll is food. Yeah, I'll eat a roll, if I'm hungry. But it ain't exactly my first choice.

Then again, sometimes it's the friend you're not that close to who you can be the most honest with, and who'll be the most honest with you. It's not like either one of you has much to lose.

"Yo, Money."

"Yo, Claude."

"Question for you."

"Hit me."

"This sick girl, Alma Lingonberry, with the friends and the yadda yadda?"

"Ah, *sí*. Flawless scam. Wish I'd thought of it first. I'm working on my own version, but I'm gonna wait till people get bored and are ready for a new dying kid. Hang on a sec, Claude—Uncle Sal, get away from my pancakes!"

Money hung up.

Whatever. Of course he'd say it's a scam. I'd suspected Alma from the beginning too. But when you actually had a conversation, she seemed cheesy, not psycho. Then again, wasn't that exactly why I'd called Money? So somebody'd tell me, *Snap out of it!*

Should I tell him about my parents and the flyers? I wasn't sure. I just knew I needed to keep talking. I was calling him back when I got a text.

MONEYMAN: sorry c, too loud here for a convo

ME: how do u know alma not real?

MONEYMAN: she SO ain't real

ME: right but how do u KNOW, tho

MONEYMAN: takes 1 2 know 1

ME: so u DON'T know, is what yr saying

MONEYMAN: not what i'm saying at all!

ME: doesn't ask for money, though. doesn't ask for anything

MONEYMAN: doesn't have to. that's the beauty of it!

Fine.

ME: so who do u think she is?

MONEYMAN: someone smart that i am jealous of

I tapped my phone on my knee. A lanky guy and his dachshund were strolling down the sidewalk across the street. A dust ball made entirely of candy wrappers followed them.

I sighed. Maybe if I told Money what I saw without going into detail, he'd give me an idea I hadn't thought of yet.

ME: listen. i saw somebody plastering BQE w/ alma flyers in middle of the night

MONEYMAN: BOOM. there's your alma

ME: maybe NOT, tho

MONEYMAN: i guess? but most likely

ME: say it's not that person, tho

MONEYMAN: why make things complicated,
claude? case cracked. take the rest of the day off!
east river's full of bluefish ready to bite

Whatever, Money. My parents wouldn't send me messages pretending to be a dying kid. They weren't *creepy*.

I was starting to worry about something else, though.
Phil always said Dad would ruin Grandpa's business.
Maybe Dad knew he wasn't a natural-born gangster
(even if, technically, he was), so he wasn't even trying to
go around being intimidating like Grandpa. Instead he
was running a moneymaking scam. In that case, Dad
wouldn't have to be the one writing the e-mails. He was
absolutely the type of person who would do the boring
parts, like posting flyers.

But that didn't explain Mom. Mom never did sketchy
stuff. It might sound surprising, with her family, but
it's true. Before beauty school, she studied phlebotomy
at community college. I didn't even know what that
was, except you got to poke people with needles, which
seemed appropriate. She'd just changed her mind about
every career she'd started so far.

Nothing made sense.

ME: i gotta find out who alma is, asap

MONEYMAN: gotta go claude! c u lata!

ME: wait!

MONEYMAN: gotta run babe

ME: not yr BABE. and wait! need help!

MONEYMAN: PEACE

ME: where are you going?

MONEYMAN: lala needs me

Not as much as I did, but try to tell them that. How come when two friends get romantic, they melt into one useless one?

ME: whatever, money

MONEYMAN: later

Luckily, there was still one person I could talk to. Somebody who knew my parents as well as I did. The only person I trusted enough to ask.

PHIL

When you have excluded the impossible, whatever remains,
however improbable, must be the truth.
—Sherlock Holmes, detective from a book

I jogged to the subway. On the stairs a smiley lady shoved a flyer at me—I don't think I need to mention whose face was on it, rhyming the day away. I stopped. "Where did you get this?" I asked. The lady's voice sounded like electronic chimes. "I'm a collector," she said. "Would you like another?" She pulled a fistful of flyers out of a plump plastic bag. A quick glance told me they were all on different topics—going back to college, learning to speak Arabic—and that she'd been ripping them off doors and poles for quite some time. "No thanks, lady," I said. She chimed, "Happy travels!" I handed the Alma flyer to the half-naked guy who dances on the platform and jumped on the train. As the doors closed, I heard him yell, "*Hoo-hoo!* Let's make it ten *million . . .*"

The whole ride I listened to this standing-up couple

have an argument about which one of them was getting cheated on by the other one. The girl had spiked hair and the guy had round glasses, and they were both carrying large cups of coffee.

"Every time I turn around, you're texting somebody."

"Why are you so paranoid?"

"You aren't the same person you used to be."

"What's going on with you these days?"

This conversation kept up all the way to Manhattan. I got madder and madder. How could people who were supposed to be tight still have no clue what each other was doing? I wondered if spiked hair and round glasses were both cheating, or if neither of them was. I wondered if they even liked each other.

When I got off the N train, the arguing couple did too. I jogged through the dark tunnel and took the stairs to the street two at a time to try to get away from them. At street level the light broke. As I got closer to Guillaume's, I noticed I was starving. I hadn't eaten breakfast. And . . .

Phil wasn't gonna be at the restaurant. Nobody was.

It was Sunday morning.

As I stood on Broadway, with the crowd flowing around me, my head felt blurry. My whole head. I pulled out my phone and made a call.

"Can't talk," said Money as he hung up on me.

The sun had cranked up the volume to full blast. The

reflections from the skyscrapers were too loud, too harsh. I crossed the street to get in the shade. Five seconds later I got a text.

MONEYMAN: yo sorry claude lala sittin here

ME: so?

MONEYMAN: lala doesn't know girl not real

ME: so?

MONEYMAN: don't want 2 hurt feelings

ME: why hurt feelings?

MONEYMAN: too sad

ME: ?

There was a long pause.

MONEYMAN: lala writes alma long emails

ME: what?

MONEYMAN: daily

MONEYMAN: loooooong emails

MONEYMAN: personal stuff

I stared at my phone.

ME: does alma write back?

MONEYMAN: yeah, but she keeps it vague

I wanted to grab a stranger by the collar and yell, "Do you have any idea how insane this is?!" But New York City has plenty of people doing stuff like that without me trespassing on their territory. Instead I inspected the ground for anything disgusting, found a clean spot, and stomped my foot.

ME: money. u have 2 tell lala. right now.

There was an even longer pause.

MONEYMAN: If i tell lala alma not real lala knows i break into her email = not cool

ME: not cool money!!!

MONEYMAN: can't help it! 2 interesting, keep it going for a while?

ME: money! stop breaking into lala email, do not tell lala alma not real, i tell her myself

MONEYMAN: whatever

ME: also that u spy on her email

MONEYMAN: claudissimo! claudio-rooney! i thought we were the new best buds!!!

ME: enough already ANDREW

MONEYMAN: lala mad b/c i m txting other babes, signing off, bye

ME: yr selfish!

MONEYMAN: xoxo

ME: ?!

MONEYMAN: j/k

As I headed back to the N train, I had no idea what in the name of my shady, sketchy, lawbreaking family tree I was supposed to do. I felt its branches stretching backward through criminal after criminal, across oceans, over mountains, through time. I felt its trunk sinking its roots right through the cement to the core of the earth, wrapping around it like blood vessels. Pain shot up from the soles of my feet through invisible wires, hurting my brain and my heart.

I melted into the river of people, the familiar loud and colorful river of people I loved and most likely would never know too well at all.

BRETT & ME

There is no trap so deadly as the trap you set for yourself.
—Raymond Chandler, writer

Brett's front door was locked. Mother Fingerless's garden gnome stood glued back together in the pot of dirt with the fake tree. I felt like hugging him.

"Leave my statue, bad girl," said Mother Fingerless. "What did you eat today?"

As I stepped inside, I said, "I'm full, thanks," which was almost true. Standing there next to the watercolor of the puppy dog in the heart-shaped frame while the old lady smiled down on me like a sunbeam, I had no appetite. How could I eat food cooked by somebody my parents were robbing?

"Bre-eett," yelled Mother Fingerless as she pulled the front door shut behind us.

When I got upstairs, Brett was hunched over his desk, reading a book by his metal lamp. He was wearing a green T-shirt—and glasses. Those were new. The frames had green and brown swirls.

"Sorry. I'm interrupting?" I asked.

It wasn't the philosophy book today. The cover had a picture of a guy in a fedora who looked like a private investigator.

"Nice glasses," I said.

Brett turned a page.

Behind me the poster for Brett's old-timey alien movie hung where it always had. PARALYZE THE LIVING AND RESURRECT THE DEAD! it said, above drawings of people looking ready for battle. The movie was hilarious. I understood why he loved it.

But that was eons ago.

I held out the bag I'd picked up on Eighth Avenue. "I brought fortune cookies. Since you're all into Chinese stuff now."

And also because of the letters, which I wasn't supposed to know about, and also because of writing on his stoop, which I didn't know how to talk about.

Brett kept reading.

"Listen, Brett," I said. "I know everything is . . . But you're the only one . . ." I futzed with the edge of the cookie bag. "I'm afraid Alma Lingonberry is my parents. Them and some other people—the gang, I guess. Running a moneymaking scam."

Brett talked in his usual calm voice without looking up from his book. "So you finally figured out that your father and his band of criminals invented Alma

Lingonberry to make money. Took you long enough."

"What?"

Silence.

"You *knew*?"

More silence.

"How long have you—wait. How do you know that?" I asked.

No answer.

"Brett!" I yelled.

When Brett looked up, his glasses made his brown eyes huge. "I don't see why I need to get involved."

"You don't see why you need to get involved?" I yelled. "Maybe because your *mother* crafted up a pile of thirteen thousand stuffed animals to save Alma's life! You're not concerned about that?"

Brett's glared at me with the huge eyes. "No."

"Just, *no*?"

It is amazing how long you can stare at someone and not see each other at all.

"Say something!" I said.

Brett closed his eyes. "Claudeline, I'm observing you getting out of control."

I shut Brett's bedroom door to check the mirror. I observed myself looking totally normal. In the mirror I saw Brett reading.

"Shut the stupid book!" I yelled.

Brett slapped the book on his desk and took off his

glasses. For a split second, he looked like the person I used to know. But his voice was different. It was shaking.

"My mother cried when she read that thing you wrote on our stoop. She assumed it was meant for her."

Ugh.

"Does she know it was me?"

"No, Claude, but I wouldn't expect you to understand that that isn't the point."

"Look. I am really sorry I wrote that thing, Brett. It was idiotic. It's just, you've been avoiding me like I'm contaminated! And you're the only one who understands—"

"Who understands what? Your sense of humor? Because I don't!"

I felt like I was in a subway car that was hurtling forward so fast I was missing all the stops.

"No!" I yelled. "You're the only one who understands what it's like to have a dad who breaks the law!"

Brett spit his words at me. "I understand what it's like not to have a father at all. That is something you *don't* understand."

When I opened my mouth, he cut me off.

"You've been treating me like I'm some boring loser because I found something interesting that has nothing to do with you. I only got interested in Chinese philosophies because your grandfather died. Which I'm sure you don't even realize didn't have to happen. Because you don't want to know how horrendous it is, being a so-called gangster.

So I don't want to watch you steal anymore, or get in
trouble. I don't want to help you reach your destiny, as
you call it. That makes me a bad friend? Fine."

"Well, I've been trying to tell you all summer that
I'm freaked out about the whole gangster thing! I've been
thinking a lot about it—"

When Brett laughed, it sounded like he was very far
away. Like he was laughing in another building, and closing all the windows. "C'mon," he said. "No you haven't.
You love thinking of yourself as so gangster, and you
don't have to take things seriously because your family's
so important. To you, life is just one big joke."

"Hey! I'm not like that!" I yelled.

And I knew I was right. *I am not like that.*

But I was mad. A different kind of mad than I'd been
when I wrote that idiotic thing on his stoop.

"*You think I don't know about stuff that's horrendous?*
What *you* don't understand, Brett, is that when somebody you love gets murdered, the last thing you want
to hear about is philosophy! Sometimes you even make
jokes! When you hurt so bad you can barely breathe,
you'll try anything to make it stop. And guess what?
Nothing works!"

He looked away.

I ran down the stairs and out the front door without
hearing what Mother Fingerless was yelling behind me.

LALA & ME

Poetry and letters
Persist in silence and solitude.
—Tu Fu, poet

The closer I got to Lala's, the more the air smelled like car fumes. Vehicles swooshed through the sky on the Brooklyn-Queens Expressway. The sun had vanished, and it was drizzling again, on and off. What a rainy summer. The wet streets made the city sound like it was whispering in the background. All the trucks swooshing, the buses swooshing, and the bikes.

Lala was alone on her stoop, wearing her zebra-print raincoat, writing with a purple marker in a notebook.

"Yo," I said.

"'Sup," said Lala in a sad voice.

I sat next to her. "What are you writing?"

Lala put the cap on her marker and stuck it in her hair. "A poem for my dad."

We sat listening to the traffic above us. I could almost see the black exhaust fumes soaking into the buildings and trees, making them sick. This part of the neighbor-hood feels extra depressing sometimes. Stuck here soak-ing up evil fumes.

"I'm sorry about your dad, Lala," I said.

"Writing poems is the best thing with that, lately," said Lala.

"It helps?" I asked.

Lala half smiled at me. I half smiled back.

We looked at our feet. Lala had on black sneakers and white socks. I had on my pink sandals and red socks. Our shoes were exactly the same size.

"Lala, we gotta talk about something," I said.

"No worries," she said. "I read all Andrew's texts."

I looked up. "So you know Alma isn't real?"

"Well . . ." Lala stretched her legs and set her note-book beside her on the stoop. "I know she's *supposedly* not real. I kind of don't believe it, though. If it's true, it's too embarrassing. That girl acted like she liked me."

"Everybody likes you, Lala," I said.

"Nobody knows the real me," said Lala.

"You're Barba Amarilla! Who doesn't know that?"

"Nobody knows I'm a *poet*." When Lala glanced at me, her gold-brown eyes reminded me of autumn leaves. Same as her mother's. She talked slowly, while she untied and retied her sneakers. "I sent her my poems."

"Really?" I said.

"And Alma said she thought they were amazing," said

166

Lala. "She made me feel like, yeah, maybe I *am* a real poet. Like I keep telling everybody. Now I just feel dumb."

"Alma being fake doesn't change that you're the best poet in this whole city," I said.

Lala looked up from her sneakers and smiled through her squiggly hair. "You haven't read my poems."

"I would if you showed them to me!"

"Alma is a poet too, though," said Lala, leaning back on the stoop again and looking across the street. "So she knows what she's talking about."

The way Lala kept calling Alma "Alma," I could tell she hoped Money was wrong. That there was some chance Alma could still be who she said she was.

I sighed. "Lala, I gotta tell you two more things."

She leaned away from me. "Okaaay . . ."

"Number one is I wrote her too," I said. "Alma. About personal stuff."

Lala smacked my arm. "You told everybody she was faking it!"

"That's what I thought! Until she wrote me back," I said, rubbing my arm. "You're brutal."

"You're gonna have a bruise," said Lala. "So what happened?"

"I don't know. From the first message, I could tell Alma was just some . . ." I tried to remember what it was about that first message that made me think Alma might be real. It wasn't anything in particular.

"Cheesy girl, right?" said Lala, smiling.

"Boring, even," I said.

"Oh, Claude." Lala pulled her marker out of her hair. "We should've been talking to each other instead of some stranger off the street. What's up with us?"

"I don't know, Lala. But I have to tell you the other thing." I closed my eyes and listened to the city whispering. "I think Alma Lingonberry is my parents."

"Huh?" said Lala.

I opened my eyes and pointed at her. "But they're not writing those e-mails. They wouldn't do us like that."

Lala scrunched her nose. "*Seriously?* Your *parents?*"

I nodded and waited to see what kind of face she would make next, to see if she already knew or had suspected. But I couldn't tell anything from Lala's face; it looked like maybe she wasn't sure.

Lala took the cap off her marker and put it back on. "Your family does have issues."

"Ya think?" I said.

She looked at me sideways. "How do you know this, Claude?"

"I saw Dad posting Alma flyers under the BQE. And my mom had a bunch of them in her purse. Somebody else has to be writing the e-mails, but you know—it's called organized crime. Maybe my parents organized it."

"I don't know your mother too well, but to me, this

doesn't feel like the type of thing your pops would do," said Lala. "I'm all confused right now, though, and I hear you. So let's say he *is* being Alma. We *will* get wild on him. But after that, let's think about you for a second."

"Okay," I said.

Lala put her notebook on her lap and draped her arm around me. "So what? So what if your parents made up Alma to make money?"

Now I was scrunching my nose.

"Yeah, it's grimy. But does it change if they love you?" Lala held a hand out, with her palm up, like she was giving me her idea and I could take it if I wanted to. "Your pops could steal all the money in the world, but isn't he still your pops? Just saying, Claudeline."

I didn't know what to think. If my family stole all the money in the world, did it change if they loved me? I didn't know. Did it change if I loved them? I didn't know! I mean, shouldn't it?

Why couldn't my family feel like what a family was supposed to feel like? Instead of sketchy people I was stuck with. Cursed by.

I looked at the buildings across the street. One was kind of red but kind of black. The one beside it was kind of yellow but kind of black.

"I don't know how to feel anymore, Lala. But I need to know the truth."

"We're not playing games," said Lala. "We're about to crack this open."

I checked to see what kind of face she was making.

"Yes, I said *we*," said Lala.

And we hugged and snapped our fingers and made a plan.

THE PLAN

What difference between good and bad?
—Lao Tzu, philosopher

My assignment was to observe my parents for information about what they were doing, where they were going, and anything else. That night, when I heard Dad come home, I tiptoed out of my bedroom into the dark hallway and peeked through the doorway to the kitchen. Dad was using a chair as a footrest, watching music videos on his phone. His bare knees poked through the rips in his jeans.

Why would he watch videos on a phone in the kitchen when we've got a huge TV in the living room? Unclear. I stood with my back flat against the plaster, waiting for something to happen, until I was so tired of thinking about Dad and the videos—I mean, there are ways of hooking up your TV screen to the Internet so you can watch whatever you want; you don't *have* to settle for rappers with heads one centimeter tall and mouths the size of a speck of lint, unless you love being annoyed, which I didn't—I had to go to bed. I didn't bother tiptoeing down the hall.

"Good night, Claude," called Dad.

"It could go either way," I called back. Then I went into my room to put on my nightgown and try to stay awake until Mom came home. Maybe they'd let something slip about Alma when they thought I was asleep.

When I finally heard the front door unlock, I was barely awake. Mom and Dad clinked around the kitchen for a while, yammering about nothing. Eventually, I heard this:

Mom: You're supposed to be there at noon?

Dad: Anytime after noon. Why am I working with him again?

Mom: *Gotcha!*

Dad: *Gotcha!*

Mom: Head case. How you getting into Manhattan?

Dad: Car service.

Mom: I'm so tired. All this junk. Did you show him the new ones?

Dad: Come in with me tomorrow. He's constantly asking for you.

Mom: I'd rather not.

Dad: Then stop agitating and let me handle it.

Mom: *Gotcha!*

Dad: Pass me that thing with the chicken.

Besides the strange but useless fact that my parents

had a secret catchphrase, I learned that Dad was taking a car service to Manhattan sometime after noon the next day to meet somebody he was working with. Where in Manhattan I had no idea, but it was a start.

I texted Lala. She said she'd tell her mother we were selling raffle tickets for the carnival and reserve a car service for us to follow Dad. A car service is Brooklyn's version of a taxi. Instead of standing on the street waiting for a yellow cab to flag down, you call a black town car to pick you up. And town cars take reservations, which is helpful when you have to be someplace at a certain time and can't afford to spend half an hour jumping up and down on the curb, flailing your arms.

I worried about how we'd follow Dad without getting noticed, and how we'd pay for the car service, but Lala said she never worried about things like that, so I decided not to either.

I had enough to worry about.

THE CHASE

For an occurrence to become an adventure,
it is necessary and sufficient for one to recount it.
—Jean-Paul Sartre, philosopher

Our town car was waiting around the corner by the Fourth Avenue N train subway stop. Lala was sure that Dad's car would pick him up in front of our apartment, turn right, and pass us on its way to Manhattan. That's when we'd jump on his tail.

As we walked toward the subway stop, I asked, "Which car service did you call?"

"The one next door to the noodle shop. At Your Service Car Service," said Lala. "The sign says, 'It's More Than a Destination. It's a Journey.'"

"What's that supposed to mean?" I asked.

"I don't know," said Lala, "but it sounds cool, right? I always wanted a reason to call them."

As soon as we climbed into the backseat and shut the door behind us, the driver waved us out. "Oh, no you don't. I don't pick up no kids alone."

"We're not kids; we're tweens," said Lala. "And we're on a journey! I made a reservation."

"My right to refuse! I got rights. Out," said the driver.

"It's an emergency!" said Lala.

"Call an ambulance," said the driver.

"Sir," I said, "we reserved this car because of an important situation and it's—"

"Not my problem. I'm not taking no kids nowhere without an adult!" said the driver.

Me and Lala looked at each other.

"Out! Now!" The driver was wearing a patterned scarf, a cap, and reflecting sunglasses.

Lala sniffled. Her voice quivered like she was about to cry. "It's just that someone is very sick."

"Don't know the guy," said the driver. "Outta my car."

That's when the town car with Dad inside passed us, just as Lala predicted, and stopped at the light.

I punched Lala. We ducked.

So At Your Service Car Service was next door to the noodle shop, eh?

I chewed my lip. I had an idea. The type of thing a bad guy would do. On the other hand, it was for a good cause. Did that matter? No. But Dad was getting away, and what was I supposed to do? Become an angel overnight? You shouldn't try to change all at once. You might pull a muscle. That was Chinese philosophy, I was pretty sure.

I said, "Sir, do you know Si Song?"

"The old one or the son?" said the driver.

"Senior," I said.

The driver said, "Dead."

"Oh, *really*?" I laughed.

"DEAD!" said the driver. "Dead, dead, dead."

"Sir," I said. "Do you really think . . ."

I peeked out the window. The light had turned green. Dad was getting away.

"Do you really think a man like Si Song *dies*? This is a message from my grandfather: FOLLOW THAT CAR! You don't wanna—"

"WAIT!" yelled the driver. He pointed at me in the rearview mirror. "Not dead?"

I raised one eyebrow. "I ain't said *nothin'*."

"What car? That one? That town car there?" he asked.

"That one," said Lala, pointing.

"I'm not driving no kids nowhere without an adult!" yelled our driver as he screeched into traffic and got on Dad's tail.

Have you ever seen an action movie with a thrilling high-speed car chase through the streets of New York City?

Lies. All lies. There is way too much traffic for that.

The Brooklyn Bridge was a parking lot. Through the windows I observed the gigantic sky curving around us like an upside-down bowl. It was that perfect light blue you see in picture books, with skinny clouds scribbled in white chalk.

Our town car was one of a few hundred vehicles hanging over the East River, facing off with the Manhattan skyline, waiting impatiently to step on the gas and shoot like rockets into the scene, watching the skyscrapers get bigger and bigger until we all disappeared in the maze.

Meanwhile we were more like a few hundred great-grandmothers making our way, inch by inch, from the bathroom sink—slowly, easy now—toward a painting of what? Of a skyline! Hanging way, over, there, clear, across, the room, stopping every, two seconds, to point out, how beautiful, it is. Before we get there, we're all droppin' dead.

These are the kind of thoughts a kid comes up with when she's stuck in traffic.

"Why did your Dad's car go this way?" said Lala. "He shoulda took the other bridge."

Our driver shook his head. "I bet you anything there's a young guy behind the wheel of that car. Young guys don't know nothing about New York City traffic patterns. What is GPS? Robots in space! For *years* I study human behavior—*human behavior*, for *years*—before I take even one fare. *Whaddayagonnadoaboudit?*"

Our driver's accent and appearance jumbled together made me curious where he grew up. I was considering whether there was a non-none-of-your-business way to ask about somebody's family tree when, out of nowhere, the dam broke, the traffic flowed, and we were off.

Lala and I slammed against the backs of our seats, then sideways against the door as the driver shifted lanes to stay on Dad's tail.

I wondered when would be the best moment to break it to him that we were somewhat short on cash.

The windows were down. The breeze was hot. The city was alive. Not too loud, not too dull. Alive. Our town car's idling engine rumbled like a purring lion. We were parked outside some beauty salon, waiting for Dad. What was he doing inside a beauty salon? Wouldn't we like to know. But there was no way Lala and me could get out of the town car to spy without getting caught. We'd just have to hope he came out with somebody, or something, that would give us another clue. Whatever Dad was up to in there, it was taking an awful long time.

While we waited, I imagined we were the cement lions outside the New York Public Library, ready to pounce. The picture was clear: Lala was Lala, only with a cement mane and sunglasses and a long tail, and I had paws as big as my head. Agim was there, too—Agim, you know, our driver? Only he was a jaguar, prowling back and forth in front of a window display of severed hands decorated with nails in every color in the galaxy, plus a few colors that only exist inside beauty salons. Looking back, I guess I was half-asleep and dreaming.

"I add turmeric. That's key," said Agim—the human version, who was still sitting behind the wheel and shaking his pointer finger at Lala.

"No doubt?" said Lala.

"Think I'm joking? Try my chicken," said Agim.

"Chicken with biscuits is great," I said.

"Biscuits, blech. Rice!" said Agim. "You don't know nothing from my chicken."

"Oh, Agim, I wish we had some now," said Lala. "I'm dyin' here."

"Be our guests any Sunday, girls," said Agim. "Lala, bring your mother and the boys. She needs rest, your mother, all she's been through." Agim leaned forward and pointed out the window. "Hey! This guy of Si's, he takes care of himself."

Dad and his new hairstyle got into his town car.

"He got layers framing his face!" said Lala.

"Dad was *getting his hair done*?" I said.

We knocked around the backseat like two Ping-Pong balls in a Lotto machine until we hit the next light. This thing with the lights happened approximately twenty-five more times before we arrived at what turned out to be Dad's real destination. By that time, our car chase had taken almost two hours.

* * *

In the end, we learned what we needed to know.

We were parked outside a humongous building downtown. Agim was leaning his whole body out the car window, talking with an enormous security guard. They were speaking a language I had never heard before and have never heard since and shaking each other's shoulders and tipping their hats and it seemed like they had known each other since the day they were born.

Agim pulled himself back inside the town car. "You ask any Albanian in New York City and he's not gonna lie. He's gonna tell you. And it all equals out in the end."

I'd completely lost track of this conversation, and I had no idea where we were, or where Dad was. Albania? Was Dad in Albania? I felt like I'd been awake for three days.

Lala leaned forward. "What's the scoop, Agim?"

"Your father—Claudeline? Is she awake, our sleeping one?" said Agim.

"I'm up," I said.

"Claudeline, this place is the FBI. Your father is a rat. He's giving up Si Song Senior."

Whoa. A *rat*?

"A rat?" said Lala.

"An informant," said Agim. "Si Junior works for the government now. Full-time. My lips are sealed and you didn't hear it from me."

"I think your pops might be too busy to be writing poetry," said Lala.

Dad was telling the FBI about Grandpa?

What was he telling them?

I put my hands over my face. This was not good.

Was it?

"So Claudeline, where to?" asked Agim.

I frowned. "Albania."

"Back to Brooklyn," said Lala. "Thanks, Agim."

"This one's on me," said Agim. "No money, I don't take it. Every Sunday, girls, my wife makes a feast. Lala, you tell your mother she brings nothing. Nothing but her family. We'll have a wonderful time. And hey, Claude, I wish you the best of luck with whatever this situation is that you got going on here."

"Thanks, Agim," I said.

"And the bad guys? May they choke on their meatballs. Tell 'em that's from Agim."

Our heads slammed forward, then backward, as we spun around and made our way across the bridge back home.

RATS

Buffalo wings = chicken wings in spicy sauce.
World = full of lies.
—Steve Martin, comedian

At Guillaume's, Phil and Rita made background noise while I kicked the bar and thought about rats. Liars and fishy schemers and rats. Rats carry diseases. Rats infest kitchens. Sure, some people keep rats as pets, but is that normal?

Lala was right. If Dad was ratting to the FBI, he probably wasn't pretending to be a sick girl to raise money. That'd mean he was breaking the law right under some FBI agent's nose. But if my parents weren't Alma, who was? And what were they doing with the flyers?

I was dying to see what Phil made of this situation, but I'd watched enough movies to know that a gangster getting cozy with the FBI ain't the type of thing you wanna spread around. I felt lost.

Somebody tickled my ear.

"I must run," said Rita. "Tell me I'll see you at the Sunset Park carnival this weekend?"

Rita was as swanky as ever in a white pantsuit and a necklace made of lavender rocks. Her mouth was open waiting for my RSVP. Her silver tooth looked overly enthusiastic to me.

"Isn't Sunset Park sorta unfancy for you, Rita?" I asked.

"It's research for my screenplay!" said Rita.

A movie. That's what I needed. A break from kid-detective land and its forests full of giant magnifying glasses. "How's that going, anyway?" I asked.

Rita unbuckled her white leather bag, pulled out a stack of paper, and handed it over with a smile. "I've got fifty pages!"

I flipped through them. "'GRANDPA RICARDO: You dirty rat-a-tat-tat! You want a belly fulla lead?'" I nodded. "Not bad."

Rita's smile fell. "But I want it to be bad. Good-bad, like you said."

"The carnival should give you some ideas," I said. "We got lotsa characters in my neighborhood."

"You kids have a ball without me," said Phil.

"You won't be there?" asked Rita.

"Nah," said Phil. "Gotta visit my no-good brother-in-law and my angel niece over in Jersey. A day trip outta the neighborhood keeps a guy alert."

"Where do you live, anyway?" I asked. I thought of Phil as living in taverns and restaurants. I knew he lived in Sunset Park—behind a bar was just the only place I'd ever seen him.

"Over there by Green-Wood Cemetery," said Phil. "They call it 'South Park Slope' now, trying to get the fancy-pantses we serve in here to buy buildings out there. Ain't gonna stick, though. We got ghouls scarin' 'em off."

"Bring your brother-in-law and his daughter to the carnival!" said Rita.

"I'll think about it," said Phil. As we waved goodbye to Rita, Phil raised a tangled eyebrow at me, and I smiled. He was done thinking about it.

As soon as Rita sashayed away, a man decked out in a peach suit edged onto her empty stool. Meanwhile, Mom was speeding around the dining room in her red dress and red heels like a fire truck. I'd been so lost in rat city, I hadn't noticed that the restaurant was getting slammed.

"Mom's getting a workout tonight," I said.

"Sara hates this job," said Phil. He kept a tray of glasses filled to the brim amazingly steady as he passed it to a waiter. "But what's she gonna do? She's got no experience. Guillaume only hired her 'cause I begged him. Between you, me, and the fence post, it helps that your mother looks like a cross between Ava Gardner, Angelina Jolie, and what God dreams up when he's makin' his coffee. But I tell you what, we get a hundred fashion models in here every week carryin' their résumés like they're tickets to the prom."

"I'm surprised you wanted to work with her," I said. "She's even meaner to you than she is to me."

"Your mother and me are like family, Claude—we've known each other too long. Okay, I confess. Getting her hired wasn't *that* hard. Guillaume thinks he oughtta be rubbin' elbows with—how do you wanna call it?— *underworld celebrities*." Ice cubes clinked as Phil dropped them in glasses. He lowered his voice. "That's why he hired me. For my *authenticity*. You believe that? He wanted dirt from the streets. Loves bragging to his rich customers that his barkeep here was pretty well con- nected to the big guys, back in the day. He thinks that's impressive or somethin', and for this kind of money I'll put on a show. Humor him with his whaddayacallit, *authentic* Brooklyn thing, right to the bank."

"I been thinkin' a lot about who's authentic in Brooklyn myself, lately," I said.

"Yeah, Brooklyn is stylish these days. Brooklyn! Who knows why? And as long as I'm makin' this kind of money, who cares?" Phil cackled. "Guillaume's a sweet- heart. Got the backbone of a bowl of Malt-O-Meal."

The way Phil's bony fingers sped through his usual motions—mixing drinks, handing them out, grabbing napkins, reaching for limes—it looked almost auto- matic. Like his fingers could do the job without him.

"Do you need me to leave?" I asked.

"Stay!" said Phil, as he handed two cocktails to a lady with droopy shirtsleeves. "Don't leave me alone with these people. Talk to me."

Mom had said she didn't want me to become a barfly, but it was such a pleasant way of avoiding reality. I took a sip of my pineapple juice. "So you're gonna visit your niece this weekend? How come I never heard about her?"

"My niece? My niece, the niece I talk about all the time?" said Phil.

I definitely needed to become a better listener.

Phil handed a cocktail to a lady wearing an expensive-looking watch and pulled his wallet out of his pocket. He flipped open the wallet to a blurry photo of a girl younger than me who sorta resembled him. Which wasn't as scary as it sounds, but it wasn't nature giving her the greatest birthday present either. "Her ninth birthday party, over in Jersey, a couple years back. I rented a horse."

"She's my age? How come I've never met her? I *know* I'd remember that."

"You kiddin' me? My no-good brother-in-law doesn't let the kid out of the backyard. Real life's gonna be a shock for her. Gonna have to toughen up my little angel someday, but let it wait. We ain't all born into greatness like you."

"Greatness," I said. I put my toothpick in my mouth and chewed it. I felt like having a Pepe Renaud moment, pounding the bar and barking in my perfect French, "My grandfather was a thief! My father is a rat! You call that born into greatness? I call that born into a pack of snivelin' snails!" But since I speak even less French than I do Chinese, I probably would've just yelled, *"Escargot!"* Which is French for snails, which in a joint like this would've ordered me a side dish.

Phil flipped his wallet shut and held up a finger to a customer who was trying to get his attention.

"Sir," called another customer in a fake-polite voice. "Can I get some help here?"

"Maybe you better run after all, Claude," muttered Phil. "The liberal elite want Bellinis and mochatinis and all the other silly cocktails that keep this place in business by the markup alone. Have fun at the carnival. Kick a clown for me."

I watched Phil lean over the bar to take an order and hopped off my stool. A carnival wasn't at the top of my list of things to do this weekend either, but I had no choice. I was helping Mother Fingerless at her stuffed-mutant table.

Which was insane!

I headed home to rustle up the rat and get some answers. I may not have known who Alma Lingonberry was, but at least I knew why I was helping Mother Fingerless help her get well soon. Which was because I'd promised the old lady I would.

What was Dad's excuse?

The rat, the rat. *Rat-a-tat-tat.*

A LIVE APPEARANCE

Faced with what is right, to leave it
undone shows a lack of courage.
—Confucius, philosopher

The rat was not in the nest. So I checked my e-mail, out of habit.

To: ClaudelineLeBernardin5@xmail.com
From: Lil.Poet123@xmail.com

Come and play a ton of games
Let's have fun and be together
We're people, all the same
Even during dark & stormy weather.
—Alma Lingonberry

THE SUNSET PARK CARNIVAL IS ALMOST HERE.
Are you coming? It's Saturday at the basilica!
Why am **I** such an eager beaver? Beca-a-ause:

My doctors are letting me drop by for *half an hour*

not even kidding

Cool, right? 1 of my friends will be selling handmade collectibles and I want 2 give her a big hug, and so should u.

Meet me:

At the craft table with the big pink flag

At 6PM

I am probably (warning) going 2 look like a ferret, all scrawny. Who cares? See u there!

And there was another e-mail, just for me.

To: ClaudelineLeBernardin5@xmail.com

From: Lil.Poet123@xmail.com

dear claude,

what's up, girl? sorry i've been gone so long. how are u? me, i'm feelin better! i even talked to my doctor about the soup smell, like u said. she couldn't fix it, but i made her laugh. maybe i'm learning something from u! also just wanted 2 add becuz i forgot. i am ***so super sorry*** yr grandpa died. altho i've never met yr grandpa, he sounds like a superstar. maybe he can live on thru u? anyways wish u were online right now. will u tell me more stories? sounds like u will b there saturday? THANK u.

embarrassing having people give me money, 2 be honest. k gotta go. can't wait 2 finally meet! can we talk in private??

xo almz

I shut my laptop, feeling seasick. I wasn't heartless. I wasn't heartless at all.

If she wasn't my parents, then couldn't Alma Lingonberry still just be some corny kid?

At least one other person needed the answer to that question as much as I did. I made a call.

"What's up with those e-mails?" asked second-grade-voice Lala. "Do you think she's really coming?"

Honestly?

I hoped so.

I'm not saying I thought so. Or that I didn't think so. I'm just telling you what I hoped.

We stuck with our plan to meet at our bench in the park on Saturday and head to the basilica together. After we hung up, I looked out my window. Since our fight, Brett's voice had been stuck on repeat in my head. For sure some of what he'd said was wrong. Like that I thought everything was funny because my family was so important. Like that I thought he was boring.

But not all of it.

Since the day we met, Brett was the one person on earth I had never had to explain my family to. I was supposed to be the same thing for him.

All summer, I'd only been thinking about myself. Not that I didn't have important things to think about. I did. But the whole time I was carrying around my photograph of the dog pile of gangsters, wishing I could find a way to talk to Brett about the Thing—the fact that my grandfather hurt people, and what to make of it—Brett had been trying to talk to me about his own life. His father, who was gone, even though he was still alive.

I'd have given anything to turn back time and listen to him.

Grandpa Si's funeral was what had gotten Brett into Chinese philosophy in the first place. The funeral program was in my desk drawer. I'd never read it. Maybe that seems strange. But this was a *funeral* program. Having Grandpa's whole life wrapped up like that, it felt too final. Like nothing new would ever happen to him. It was already all written up.

The paper was thin, with flecks of gold.

```
Min Song was born in Fuzhou, China,
the son of a fisherman known for
his elaborate tales. His mother
died in childbirth. His father never
remarried. As a young man, he came
to the United States to seek his
fortune. In New York City he was
known as Simon.
```

```
Simon was a well-respected man who
helped build thriving communities
in New York City and Fuzhou. His
sense of humor was well known, and
he loved surprising strangers with
his knowledge of many languages,
including three Chinese dialects,
English, Vietnamese, Spanish, French,
and Russian.
```

The program kept going, talking about Grandpa meeting his wife, and Dad getting born, and Dad's mom dying, and Dad marrying Mom, and finally me.

```
The way to Simon's heart was his
granddaughter, Claudeline.
```

There was a great picture of him too, all dressed up in his hat, scarf, and eyeglasses, smiling at the camera like he was about to tell you a secret. The same way he used to smile at me.

Tell me the secret, Grandpa. Tell me why you're gone.

Did you mean it when you said I should follow in your footsteps?

Tell me what I'm going to do without you.

Tell me what to do.

On the back of the program was a quote:

When the desires of men are curbed,
there will be peace,
And the world will settle down of its
own accord.
—Lao Tzu

All I had was orange construction paper, but that was fine. I took out a pencil and wrote a letter to someone who was waiting for one. I couldn't find an envelope, so I folded the letter in half. On the outside I drew one of the few Chinese symbols I know how to make, the one that means love. Before I could think twice, I left it under the bag of fortune cookies on that person's stoop.

I almost turned around and grabbed it, but I didn't. I chucked a rock at his window, and then I crossed back over the eons toward home.

I didn't feel like going inside yet, so I sat on our stoop, watching the sunset reflected off buildings and cars. The edges of the neighborhood blazed orange and gold, like the sun wanted to remind everybody, *Don't forget: I'm a big ball of fire.*

The funeral-program version of Grandpa's story matched the one I liked telling myself. He traveled around the world talking to people in all different languages. He helped build thriving communities.

But there were some key details that version of the story left out.

When I'd looked the Thing in the eye that night in the park, the truth about it had flooded into me and washed my brain clean. To defeat it, I couldn't play its game. I had to starve it of light, and breath, and getting its photo taken.

I didn't know anymore if I was a bad kid, a good kid, or plain old Claudeline, but I could tell you this much. If I was the Thing, I would not want me as its enemy. People in my family don't go down without a fight. We swing first.

And my version of swinging first was gonna be not swinging at all. It might not be what Grandpa meant by me taking over his business, but I was the one calling the shots now.

I wrapped my arms around my knees and looked at the sky, at the rooftops that went on and on, making a patchwork of shapes to cover so many lives, so many lives you could keep yourself busy forever trying to imagine all of them. In a city like this, I wasn't doomed. I was sure of it.

SCOTT JONES

The sage is guided by what he feels and not by what he sees.
—Lao Tzu, philosopher

Carnival day was hot. The kind of hot that makes your eyes burn. When I got to the top of the hill in the park, somebody was already sitting on our bench, somebody who resembled an Antarctic bird stranded in the wrong climate. I hadn't said anything about meeting up in my letter—Lala must have invited him. I wasn't sure I was ready to face Brett yet. I strongly considered turning back and running a few miles to the edge of the borough and over the Verrazano Bridge. I saw no reason why I shouldn't start a fantastic new life on Staten Island.

Money clomped up the hill from his side of the park. He was wearing khaki pants and a red Hawaiian shirt with those mushy brown shoes dudes wear on yachts, carrying a cardboard box with shells and balls sliding around inside and panting like he was all out of breath.

"No way, Andy," said Brett. "A shell game? Are you setting that up at the carnival?"

"If Lala's forcing me to be here, the least I can do is make it profitable," said Money. "Uncle Sal turned the dining room table into a taco bar! Do you have any idea what I'm missing?"

A shell game is a classic big-city rip-off. A guy hides a ball under some shells and moves the shells around. People bet money on where the ball is. No matter how closely you watch the shells, you can't find the ball, so the guy takes your money. If the cops come, the guy cleans up the game and disappears into the crowd. It's one of the oldest tricks in the book.

Lala ran toward us, coughing. She wore a sundress with huge orange flowers, sunglasses, and a braid like the one Alma wore in the drawing on her flyers. She plopped on the bench beside Brett and sniffled. "Excuse me; I'm getting sick. Nice glasses, Brett."

When Money dropped his box, the balls and shells clunked. "You don't sound sick, babe."

"You best believe I'm sick," said Lala.

"Are you pretending to be sick to compete with Alma?" asked Brett.

"Listen. If that girl exists, she's about to find herself in a freestyle battle. Then we'll see who can rhyme. And she's not winning just because people feel sorry for her. Have you ever heard of leveling the playing field? They do it in sports." Lala sniffled again. "Anybody got a tissue?"

Brett tried to catch my eye.

I pretended that my fingernail was fascinating. "Lala, you're losing it," I said.

"We all know you ain't sick, babe," said Money. "And we all know Alma ain't sick. Let's hope whoever shows up puts on a better act than you. Gotta keep people amped about helping sick kids. Mine's a dude. Scott Jones. No diagnosis yet. I'm gonna drop the hammer when this Alma thing blows over. He's got three hundred fifty friends and counting. I stay in constant contact with them. I'm building relationships. Well, Scott is."

"Scott Jones?" I said.

"People ain't smart enough to investigate, they deserve to get ripped off," said Money.

"Excuse you?" said Lala.

"Is it Alma's fault you guys were so desperate that you forced her to listen to your drama?" said Money.

"Real nice, Andy," said Brett.

"If you're so sure Alma doesn't exist, Money, why do you keep calling her *Alma*?" I asked.

"Shorthand," said Money. "What should I say? The person or people pretending to be Alma probably wish they were flipping burgers instead of scrolling through your incomprehensible chick problems? Waste of breath."

Lala took off her sunglasses and glared at Money. "I *like* writing down what's in my heart. I actually feel better after I write to that girl, even if she *doesn't* exist.

And I'm starting to get a certain feeling about you, Scott Jones. A bad feeling."

"On that note: Being," said Brett, "is born of not being."

He handed each of us a slip of paper. I was still too nervous to look at him. But he was really trying, which was a good sign . . .

That's all it said: *Being is born of not being.* I checked the other side—nothing.

While everybody read the message, birds tweeted summer songs. A group of girls playing soccer thwacked the ball and grunted.

I got the feeling nobody had a clue what this meant.

Well, I hadn't understood what Brett was about for a long time. It was going to take me a while to catch up. If he wanted me to catch up.

"'Being is born of not being,'" said Lala. "I like that, I think. What does it mean?"

"It sounds like a business philosophy," said Money. "I'm getting pumped about seeing this in poster form, something I could sell online to other business dudes, but I have no idea what it means, so tell me in five words or less."

Brett pushed his glasses up his nose. "Something like trust your gut."

"Ew," said Lala. "That means trust your intestines. What do they know? Besides, my intestines are about to get busy with some food-truck junk! No, seriously, I like it, Brett. It's poetry." She folded her note into an accordion and glued it to her bottom lip with her spit. "Look, Claude. I got a beard. Like that dude who makes the peanut-butter noodles."

I snickered.

"Lala—c'mon," said Brett. "It means you have to stop thinking about yourself for long enough to experience the world around you. Stop wanting everything to be different from how it is. You have to be someplace, just be there, and feel what it feels like. And that's when you know."

"Know what?" asked Money.

"How things actually are," said Brett.

Lala twanged her paper beard, which made it fall on the ground.

"Never mind," said Brett.

"I'm sorry, Brett," said Lala. "I'm not trying to be rude. I'm still thinking about what you said. It's kind of confusing."

"Look. I'm just trying to tell you what *I'm* gonna do," said Brett. "What I think might help us figure out what is up. We have no idea who Alma is. We need to observe the situation carefully, without interfering, to establish the facts."

I felt Brett look at me again. I'd mentioned the FBI in the letter. Not because of me. So he'd know my parents might not be Alma. Brett was almost never wrong about things, but this time it seemed like he was, and I knew he'd want to know about it. Having his facts straight is the most important thing in the world to Brett. He loses patience when people ignore information that doesn't fit their version of a story. I also told him about my parents and the flyers, because that piece was still confusing. And I knew Brett would want *all* the facts, not just some of them.

Brett went on. "We don't know who'll show up to meet Alma, or who'll show up to be her. Say some girl shows up and introduces herself as Alma Lingonberry. If she seems legit—fine. Great. But say you guys don't like how she looks, or talks. Say she doesn't seem sick. She seems like a scam artist to you. Don't . . . don't . . ."

"Don't what, man?" said Money.

"Don't immediately start a riot!" Brett pulled on his curls to calm down. "I'm saying people have invested a lot in this girl. Feelings will be raw."

"Since when do you care if there's a riot, Brett, as long as the truth comes out?" asked Lala.

When I looked up, Brett was looking at me the way he used to. Like I was the only one in the world who understood what he was thinking.

For an instant I let myself look back. Then I looked down and kicked the bench: *tink, tink, tink.*

"He wants to protect his mother, Lala," I said.

We both did. Getting obsessed with helping Alma was probably filling the hole in the old lady's life where all the people who never helped her were missing from. Now even the person she thought she was helping might break her heart.

I hoped not.

"All I can say is I'm gonna find out who's running the sound system," said Lala, twisting her braid.

"Why do you need to know that?" asked Brett.

"For the freestyle battle," said Lala.

"I'm gonna scout for secret exits," said Money.

"Why?" I asked.

"In case people discover that my shell game ain't an official fund-raiser," said Money, fanning himself with his phone. "At least not for the community. Definitely not for the poetry dork."

"I'm over you, Scott Jones." Lala took off down the hill singing rhymes and dancing and coughing. Money ran to catch up with her. I followed them and heard Brett's footsteps behind me.

THE CARNIVAL

You see, but you do not observe. The distinction is clear.
—Sherlock Holmes, detective from a book

The basilica is part of the movie set of my life. From the outside, its big, round stained-glass window looks like the neighborhood's personal man-made sun. I've never been inside, but I walk past the place almost every day. On carnival day, its parking lot always feels bigger than usual, with the rides, games, and food trucks. Big enough to hold anything that might happen. I watched volunteers fill barrels with balloons, set up tents, and stock cotton-candy machines.

Money ran off to find his secret exits. Laliyah ran off to find her mother, who was the emcee.

Cutie Cat strutted up to me, and I pet her. Mrs. Ramirez must have brought her. I heard myself say, "Thass my ol' frieeend," in that goo-goo voice that automatically comes out when you talk to cats and babies. Then she headed toward Brett. Out of the corner of my eye I saw Brett pick her up, and I decided to follow a salty-sweet-fried scent wherever it led.

After I'd poured my heart out to him in that letter, saying his father was losing out on a son who would change his whole life, and that I knew—

And how much I missed sharing our observations about the world, because nobody saw things like he did—

And signed it *love*, instead of *from*, and everything—

You might be wondering why it was so important for me to get away from Brett.

Or maybe it's obvious.

Before long the carnival was in full swing, and it. Was. *Packed.* People of all shapes and sizes crammed together elbow to elbow like plastic toys in the Eighth Avenue dollar stores. Groups of grandmas in pastel outfits scuttled through clusters of businessmen in baseball hats. Mobs of laughing teenagers lifted food over each others' heads. Kids crawled through their parents' legs. Heavy, ancient-looking rides plastered with chipped paintings of clouds spilled over with screaming passengers as they spun around; carnival callers yelled, "Step right up!" through plastic bullhorns; music and lights blared.

Mother Fingerless, wearing pink lip gloss and an electric-blue muumuu, glowed like a twenty-four-hour diner behind her table, which was piled with striped, sequined, buttoned, fabric-painted, hot-glued animals like giraffe-raccoons and gopher-elephants, which existed only right here, right now, where Mother Fingerless was the ringmaster of a zoo from a science-fiction movie. Her lip gloss matched her giant pink flag, which flapped from the top of a stick stuck in a vase full of marbles. Frank Sinatra's voice poured out of her portable CD player. I made a show of pretending to steal her strongbox of money.

Mother Fingerless screeched and dropped her hot dog. She slapped my hand and shook my wrist. Her curls bounced. "Claudeline, my baby girl! You kept your promise!"

"What, you're surprised? Mother Fingerless, my fine young . . ." I bit my lip. My new goal with jokes was to make them funny to both people. I hadn't quite figured it out yet. "Friend."

She pouted. "*Friend?* Hmm. Come here, you bad kid; let me love you."

Before I could get away, Mother Fingerless smooched me on the lips.

"Enough already!" I said.

Mother Fingerless gripped my wrists like she was holding on for dear life. "Say something rude, you devil! I been lonely."

"I can't think of anything," I said.

"Of course you can!" She pounded a folding chair. "Sit!"

I sat.

"Say something!"

"Honestly, it's lovely seeing you. How are you feeling today?"

Mother Fingerless practically shoved me off my chair. "Come on, you won't be funny for me? What, you don't like me no more?" Then she smooched my forehead, and I yelped. "Mm-hm," she said. "You got a fever."

I grumbled. The only time I ever hear the word "scowling" is when a teacher is reading out loud from a tale about swashbucklers. But that's the best word to describe what my face was doing while Frank Sinatra sang about being the king of New York and I wiped lip gloss off my head with my T-shirt sleeve. I tried to stay out of kissing distance as I rearranged the pile of mutants into an attractive display.

"Hope it's not too warm for Alma," mumbled Mother Fingerless, with one eye searching the crowd. "Or too cold. Do you think she'll find my flag? What time is it?"

"It's four thirty," I said. "Hurry up, young lady! You're gonna be late for the bikini competition!"

Mother Fingerless whacked my arm. "HA!"

"Easy now," I said.

"If you're not coming around to see Brett anymore, you can still come around to see me. I miss you, and it makes me realize: You're my only daughter, Claudeline. I promise you I'm going to save your soul."

"I'm gonna round us up some customers," I said.

"Save me a salami cookie, okay? I know you're holding out on me."

Mother Fingerless laughed her saucy laugh. "I got you, baby girl."

Oh well. If the old lady couldn't save Alma, at least she'd always have me.

Mother Fingerless ran out of stuffed creatures in fifty-seven minutes flat. It turned out all I had to do was drag over potential customers. Then, with the help of Frank Sinatra, her sales pitch was irresistible. "Every single creature has its own special flaw," she'd say while she dusted dandruff off somebody's shoulder or wiped mustard out of their mustache. "They are all unique and individual. Like you." After a couple of teenagers with black lipstick bought her very last mutant, she gave me one more fat kiss on the head, and I didn't even fight it. Forget saving one dying kid. That woman is so full of hope and dreams she should have her own talk show. She could turn millions of lives around.

I took a seat in a folding chair across from the stage, where the band was gonna play, and kicked my chair. *Think, think, think.* That's what I heard when I kicked my chair. *Think, think, think.* Was somebody gonna show up that night, saying she was Alma Lingonberry? What if it was like Brett said? Some girl showed up, but she didn't seem sick. She was faking a cough, like Lala. Then what? Brett had said not to make a scene, but what if I couldn't help it?

Or what if Alma showed up, and she seemed real, and sick, but there was something about her that in person I just didn't like. Well, that wouldn't be such a big deal. At least Mother Fingerless's fund-raising wouldn't go to waste.

But what if Alma showed up, and she seemed real, and sick, and I liked her, but she didn't like me?

Or she didn't show up at all?

I looked at the note from Brett. *Being is born of not being.*

At least I still knew one thing for sure. Philosophy was invented to drive people insane.

I looked around. Next to the ring-tossing booth, a crowd nodded their heads in a regular rhythm. In the middle was Laliyah, rhyming. Wow. She was sharing her poems.

A group hooted over beside the fried-dough truck— that was Money and his shell game. Laying eyeballs on that kid outside his house felt wrong. Like seeing Santa Claus on the beach. Only he was Bad Santa, dealing broken toys from the back of some van.

Beside the dunking booth, Rita the Producer was taking notes. I'd kinda forgotten she was coming, but I was impressed. Rita was teaching me a key thing about successful Manhattan players. Once they decide to do something, they really do it.

Nearby, Mother Fingerless was dancing on her empty table. Kicking up her heels and laughing *because she was a good person*. Mother Fingerless *believed* in people. She even believed in me.

Way back by the fence was Brett, by himself, looking awkward.

Brett.

I checked my phone—five forty-five. How could I wait fifteen minutes? *Thwack, thwack, thwack* replaced *think, think, think* as I kicked my chair. My stomach cramped with twitches and stitches.

If Alma showed up, what would she do? Give a speech? Like, to everybody who came out to meet her? After that, I guessed we'd talk in private, like she said.

What if we became friends in real life? Maybe Alma could help me become a good kid. A regular, boring cheeseball, like her. And then my mother would like me better, and we'd all have dinner together, especially when Alma was coming over. And there would be more microwave popcorn and television and all that, as a family.

Or what the heck. A Broadway show.

And then, when Alma got 100 percent better, me and Lala and Brett and Money could team up with her to raise money to heal other sick kids. We'd be, like, the stars of the school or something. Helping other kids turn from bad kids into good kids.

Like heroes.

Mrs. Ramirez took the stage. Her orange suit shined in the gold light of the hot afternoon. Rico and Jamie stood next to her. It was unclear why the Ramirez boys were standing there, but they looked smooth.

"Hush, hello, good evening, hush, good evening."

When Mrs. Ramirez grinned, I grinned too. I couldn't help it. If Alma didn't show up for some reason, I'd describe the carnival in an e-mail. Maybe it'd inspire her to write a poem.

Maybe I'd write one.

Mrs. Ramirez's voice boomed through the parking lot. "I want to thank everyone in our community for contributing to this extraordinary event. Give yourselves a round of applause."

The crowd applauded. I clapped too, and kicked my chair for extra noise.

"Now," she went on. "There are a few important events on the horizon."

That's when I noticed Lala, trying to catch my eye. She was crouched near the corner of the stage, waving for me to come.

Now? I mouthed.

Lala nodded.

Cutting in front of the stage while Mrs. Ramirez had the microphone struck me as a terrible idea, so I stayed put. But Lala kept making bigger and bigger motions, like a haywire crossing guard. People were starting to look.

I sighed. *Move like a rodent, Claude. If you don't get seen, you don't get whacked . . .*

I ran in a semi-bent-over way to the stage and scuttled along the edge. Lala yanked me up and dragged me beside the porta-potty. She shoved her phone in my hand. I read out loud:

"'My heart's broken to miss the fun / Hope you are enjoying the warm sun / Please have another one / When I am well, we can have some fun. Of course I had an emergency treatment today. They said they'll let me out when I'm healed but that it doesn't look good. Enjoy the festival. I'll be fine. Promise. Love, Me. Alma.'"

"So," said Lala.

"Right," I said.

"Stupid," said Lala.

Suddenly Lala hugged me so tight she almost knocked me over.

"I'm glad you're a real person, Claude," she said into my neck.

"You too, Lala," I said, feeling exhausted.

Even at a carnival, Alma Lingonberry was the ultimate roller coaster.

MY INTESTINES

Those who overcome others are powerful;
those who overcome themselves are strong.
—Lao Tzu, philosopher

When Lala ran off to help her mom with the raffle, I wandered between rides, not ready to talk to Mother Fingerless, not ready to face Brett, hoping Rita the Producer would catch a taxi back to Manhattan, wishing I could hop a train to somewhere far away, maybe Westchester.

I was sick of this. Feeling lost and confused. Like I was getting tricked. Like I was Cutie Cat, and somebody was torturing me by waving one of those cat toys in my face just to watch me jump around. I mean—maybe cats love that.

I definitely didn't.

Now Alma was in the shadows again. What would happen next? I'd get some cheesy e-mail, asking me how I was doing? I'd tell her some more personal stuff and be all happy that somebody out there in the big sloppy world cared how I felt about everything? And then what? She'd make a plan to meet me and flake again? *But she's sick,* I'd tell myself. *You can't get mad at her for that . . .*

I went into a yellow tent. Patterned quilts hung side by side on a drooping clothesline. The chopped-up shapes and colors of the patches reminded me of a kaleidoscope. How every time you turn the lens, you see things differently.

The last time I'd dealt with something that was hiding in the shadows of my brain, it was trying to tell me that Grandpa Si probably hurt other people as much as him getting killed had hurt me. I'd had to face that shadow alone, and it was starting to look like I was gonna have to face the Alma shadow alone too. I had a hunch she never planned to step into the daylight, where I could look her in the eye.

A blue ribbon that said FIRST PRIZE was pinned to a gigantic black-and-white quilt with a perfectly symmetrical snowflake in the middle. The snowflake had twelve points. It made me think of a clock.

Somebody had sat still and worked on that thing for like a hundred years, probably. Every bit of it was perfect. Every tiny stich. One perfect thing in a world that made no sense. One place where every detail got wrapped up.

But you know what, Claude? Real life hardly ever gets wrapped up in a perfect package. And someday even this quilt will be gone. Disintegrating, and falling apart.

Nobody can stop time and weather and sweat and moths and life, just plain old life, from ruining it.

I left the quilt tent and wandered behind the Italian sausage truck. A guy blared a bullhorn in my face. "Guess your weight! Guess your age! Win fabulous prizes and raise money for the community fund!"

I ducked the bullhorn and kept walking.

Perfectness doesn't last, I thought. *Unless the perfect thing is the fact that nothing ever gets wrapped up. And everything rots and disintegrates, and new things get made all the time, and both things are always happening, at once. That's how New York City is. And what's more perfect than that?*

There was a line for the Ferris wheel. With all the commotion, nobody seemed to notice me sneak my way to the front and hop into the last open cage. Then I felt guilty about cutting and decided to hop back out.

"No standing!" said the operator. He clamped on my metal seat-belt thing, clanked the door shut, and locked it.

A Ferris wheel might be even better than an empty subway car for thinking about things you don't want to think about. For facing shadows in the late afternoon. The crackling noises the wheel made as it turned could have been coming from my own brain. I rose higher and higher above the parking lot, so high I felt like I could finally see clearly.

Like I could trust my gut.

Imagine it is you. There you are, just you and your je ne sais quoi, and all this blank space on a screen in front of you, and a nice person you've never met sending you messages saying *Tell me everything about yourself.*

Would you do it?

Of course not. But say you did.

Why would you do that?!

I'll tell you why. Because you feel like talking to somebody.

Maybe nobody knows the real you anymore. Not even you. Maybe you want to test out some new versions of yourself and see how it feels. Maybe, just maybe, to part of you it doesn't even matter who is listening.

But it did matter. It mattered who was sending those e-mails. Who was taking Mother Fingerless's money. Who was reading Lala's poetry.

That's what I could see from the top of the Ferris wheel.

It mattered. What was in my heart, and who I shared it with.

It mattered who I chose to call a friend.

The Ferris wheel creaked slowly, lowering me toward the parking lot. The crowd came into focus. I might never know the whole story about Alma Lingonberry, or about anything else in my life. The details might not get wrapped up in a perfect package. But I finally felt like I had nothing left to hide, and, in a deeper way, like nothing was hidden from me.

Being is born of not being.

And speaking of not being . . .

When I got off the ride, Lala and Brett were waiting.

"Why were you on the Ferris wheel?" said Lala.

"Because it's rad," said Brett, inspecting it.

Lala frowned. "Too bad Alma had to miss all this. If she's back to being real, I mean."

"She's not real, Lala," I said. "There was no emergency treatment."

Lala played with Brett's message like she'd been having a conversation with it. "I know."

A salsa band started to play.

Brett cleared his throat. "We'll meet at the park at noon tomorrow."

"Sorry, Brett. I'm not gonna feel like hanging out," said Lala.

"We're not going to hang out," said Brett. "We're going to figure out how to catch the jerk who's ripping off my mother."

I looked up.

"Can I walk you home, Claude?"

Sometimes you gotta figure out who your friends are. Other times the answer is right in front of you, looking at you with highly magnified brown eyes.

However, when the king penguin smiled our private smile, I couldn't smile back.

I just couldn't.

Brett fidgeted with his backpack, pulling on loose threads. "Thank you for your letter. It was my fault, though. Definitely."

My cheeks felt like they were filling with warm water. "No it wasn't, Brett," I said.

Brett took my hand and nudged me with his elbow. "It doesn't matter, Claude. Let's go home."

I was so relieved, I started crying. *Really* crying.

"Aw!" said Lala, scooping us into a squishy group hug. "I never even knew you broke up!"

TRUE FRIENDS

*We don't set out to save the world; we set out to
wonder how other people are doing and to reflect on
how our actions affect other people's hearts.*
—Pema Chödrön, teacher

As I walked up our hill yet again on Sunday, I was so
happy to see his penguin head from the back, I almost
ran. Toward Brett this time, not Staten Island.

He felt me coming and turned around. I waved with
four fingers, and I had a big cheesy grin, and he broke
into one too, with his dimples, the craters on the face of
the man in the moon.

We didn't say anything right away. For now it was
enough to sit together on our bench without being
annoyed. Just being friends again, watching Manhattan
from our side of the river. True friends who understood
each other even when we didn't.

When Lala showed up, she plopped on the bench beside
me. "Andrew couldn't make it."

Brett and I exchanged a look.

"How did you get that boy to leave his house to come to the carnival?" I asked.

"I threatened to break up with him," said Lala.

Brett laughed his deep laugh. "You two have such a healthy dynamic." Then he opened his mouth like he was gonna keep talking, looked at me, looked at Lala, and groaned.

"Whoa. Am I observing that you're maybe gonna hurl?" I asked.

Brett scrunched his eyes closed, like it was gonna hurt to talk. "You guys, I have to tell you something."

Lala put her hands on my knees and leaned over my lap to see Brett better. "Oh my goodness," she said. "You're Alma."

Brett opened his eyes. "Yeah, Lala. I'm Alma. No— listen. My ma doesn't even have e-mail. I've been helping her send Alma money from the library computers."

"*What?*" we said.

I added, "Even though you thought Alma was my dad?"

"Weirdly, that made it easier," said Brett. "I told myself that when I finally got the nerve, I'd tell your father I knew what he was up to, and get Ma's money back."

"If you knew Alma was fake, why did you help her send the money in the first place?" asked Lala.

"Ma is such a handful when she's lonely," said Brett. "She'd get giddy every time she clicked send to give Alma thirty-five bucks. Once, she even kissed a librarian."

"The one with the turquoise hair?" I asked.

"How did you know that?" asked Brett.

I shrugged.

Brett moaned. "What's wrong with me?"

"Nothing's wrong with you, Brett," said Lala.

"But why did you think Alma was my father in the first place?" I asked.

"I'm not sure," said Brett. "It happened sometime around when I decided all criminals are identical. They never get better. They get worse. They do one thing wrong, justify it by saying they deserve whatever they took, or that they're helping their family, or their country, or whatever. They decide not to feel what it feels like to take advantage of people, so they can keep doing it. Eventually, they can't feel anything at all. Even for their own son."

When I thought about what to say, I realized that having a father who isn't around is probably like having a person you love who is dead. What people say doesn't help much. What helps is when they listen.

The way Brett pressed his lips together, his dimples looked extra deep. "Even though I've never met him, I've always been sure my father is the same as me. He wants to be happy. He just went the wrong direction and couldn't figure out a way back. My Chinese philosophy book says we're all connected, struggling with the same types of problems. We're not that different. So I've been sending it to him, some philosophy. The parts I think he could relate to. But he's never written me back. Not once. It hurts."

"Of course it does," said Lala.

Brett looked toward the Manhattan skyline. "And then I get this letter from my father's mother. I was hoping I could at least get to know her. But my grandmother told me to stop *harassing* her. She said I didn't exist to her. I don't *exist*."

I felt an ocean rise up in my chest. "That's . . ."

"Yeah. Horrible. So I decided to stop wasting my time on hopeless people. Fathers, colonialists, you know . . . you, Claude . . ." He looked at me, then back at Manhattan. "Everybody."

Brett's situation was different from mine, and mine was different from Lala's, but we all had one thing in common. Something had happened that had showed us that life could be extremely unfair. But if we only thought about the unfair parts, we'd get lost. We had to focus on the parts of ourselves that could bounce back from anything.

From *anything*.

"I should've thought about the bigger picture, with Ma," said Brett. "How many people are getting taking advantage of? Say whoever is being Alma has, you know, twenty or thirty people sending cash on the regular. Or more."

"We still don't know what my parents are doing with her flyers," I said.

"Sometimes I feel like this whole world is mangy," said Lala. "Where do we even start?"

We walked across the park under thick knots of tree branches. When we left on Forty-Fourth Street, the sidewalk felt sturdy underneath my feet. I knew that if we just kept going, the sidewalks of Brooklyn would keep being there, supporting us. No problem.

"We start here," I said.

Brett nodded. "The journey of a thousand miles begins with a single step, right?"

Lala grabbed his elbow. "Is that Chinese philosophy?"

Brett shrugged.

"I get it!" said Lala.

"Me too," I said. "What's happening?"

Brett tried to smile but ended up frowning at his sneakers.

I nudged him. "You wanted your mother to be happy, Brett. There's nothin' wrong with that."

"I feel like an idiot," he said.

"Feeling like an idiot is a regular part of life," I said. "That's my philosophy."

Brett gave me the penguin eye. "Kinda deep."

"Maybe I'll write you a philosophy book," I said. "And put that in it. Along with never let your mother talk to strangers online."

Brett burst out laughing, which made me think I was getting the hang of joking around about touchy subjects. Anyway, a laugh ain't a bad sign.

As we walked along together, we decided that our next step was figuring out what my parents were doing with those Alma flyers, once and for all.

With or without the giant magnifying glass, it was unavoidable: I was officially a kid detective. And it was time for me to conduct some tough interviews. First up was the maître d' with the bad attitude who'd given me the slip one too many times already. After that I'd pay a visit to the gangster who was getting cozy with the FBI. Outsmarting my parents wasn't gonna be easy, but last time I checked, easy wasn't part of the job description.

WATCH WHERE YOU STEP

Know thyself, know thy enemy.
A thousand battles, a thousand victories.
—Sun Tzu, philosopher

When I got to Guillaume's, it was late afternoon. The front door was still locked, so I cut through a dark, stinky alley and slipped through the side door to the kitchen.

Cooks wearing white jackets and orthopedic shoes chopped meat, boiled bones, and twirled around each other like dancers with knives on a stage of smoke and flames. Chef Guillaume stood beside a woman covered with vegetable tattoos. He opened his arms wide. "*Comment ça va*, Claudeline?"

"Hunky-dory," I said. "You?"

Guillaume puffed his cheeks. "Stress, always, suffering. But no matter. My soul has developed a taste for misfortune. That's Camus. French philosophy, hmm?"

"That stuff'll kill you, Guillaume."

"Stress, yes, I know it," he said.

"Not stress," I said. "Philosophy."

I pushed open the double doors to the front of the house (that's "dining room," in restaurant lingo) and observed. Dim lights. Empty tables. My mother, sitting on the banquette (restaurant lingo for "padded bench"), rubbing leather menu covers with oil.

I took a seat across from her and played with the white flower in the glass vase.

"'Sup, Mom," I said.

Observe Mom, zapping me with her eyes like they're a metal detector. "Who wants to know?"

Me, playing it casual. "Oh, nobody. Hey, I just thought of something. You know that neighborhood girl who is sick? Astrid, or Ant-face, or whatever?"

"You don't know her name?"

"Allison?"

Mom, rolling her eyes. "Why are you so fascinated with this subject? There are people in this world who pretend to be something they are not, because they are slime! What else I can tell you?"

Me. *"Huh?"*

Mom, wiping under her eye like she's fixing a makeup problem: "Tired of thinking about this junk already today."

Me. "Wait. What are you saying?"

Mom. "What did I say?"

"Are you telling me you're not friends with Alma Lingonberry?" says me.

"I am reiterating to you that *there is no such person,*" says Mom.

"You know Alma isn't real?" I yell.

"How many times have I told you that?" is what Mom yells back.

"You have definitely *never* told me that!" yells me.

"Well, how obvious is it?" yells Mom. "What, it's not obvious?"

Me, forcing a laugh that I can only describe as sounding like a fake poet fake dying. "Of course it's obvious! I'm just *saying*! So why do you always have her flyers? And—"

Mom, stopping me with her hand. Her wedding ring, catching the light, shooting it another direction. "I remove those eyesores from the streets. But—*as you know*—somebody in our family spends a fair amount of time stealing them from me. Half paranoid I see 'em back out on the same poles I snatched 'em off of, but that seems like an awful lot of effort for you."

Observe my brain, break-dancing out of the restaurant, down the street, up an imaginary fire escape into the clouds.

Me, saying, "Dad."

Mom, folding napkins: "Dad what?"

"Dad's been—" *Dad's been taking your flyers, without telling you.* I don't even believe myself.

Mom, looking down her long nose and arching her eyebrows: "Right, Claude. *Dad's* been taking the flyers I've been ripping down every night on my way home from work. Not you. Well then, I guess I'll talk to *Dad* about leaving my stuff alone. Seriously can't figure out what your obsession is with this, Claude. It's not like you're the type those slimeballs target."

Target? Who is Alma Lingonberry, a sniper?

I can't resist. "What type of person do they target?"

"Lonely individuals," says Mom. "Highly sheltered people who've got no clue how life is in the streets."

The first time I open my mouth, all that comes out is a sigh. Where to begin, with that comment?

Me, putting my head in my hands. "So who's doing this, Mom? *Who is Alma Lingonberry?* It's back to being Dad. But then again, it ain't Dad, seeing as how he's a rat and whatnot . . ."

Mom, slowing down. "What do you know about rats?"

Me, backing up. I don't wanna tell her I've been spying on Dad yet. Not until I know more.

"Dad's a rat, you know? Like a dude who keeps the night owls company? Fat, beady-eyed? King of the rodents?"

"What night owls?" says Mom, and then, "Wait. Who's fat? *Dad?*"

Which I pretend not to hear, and the rats trail off into the long, mixed-up night.

"Listen, Claude," says Mom, flipping her hair. "Slimeball scam artists have been around since the dawn of time. And they're always fishing. Stay outta their nets."

"Thanks for the warning," I say.

"No problem," says Mom, looking satisfied.

Let us now collect our observations and examine them.

Mom only had Alma flyers because she was taking them off the streets. It's gonna take a while to adjust to this information, because it is insane.

My language arts teacher used to tell us, "Say everything as clearly as you can." My mother must've gone to one of those low-performing schools where they tell everybody to talk in circles until the people around them are as hurt and confused as possible.

What we're left with are two questions: Why would Dad take Mom's flyers? And why wouldn't he tell Mom he was doing it? Out of the corner of my eye we observe Phil, walking into the restaurant, wiping rain droplets off his bald patch. Phil could help us make sense of this, if we could get him to talk without accidentally mentioning rats. I decided to conduct another interview, on the fly.

Mom neatened her stack of polished menus. She already looked tired, and the restaurant wasn't even open yet. For once she reminded me more of a mother than a fashion model.

"I'm gonna get some clams before we open," said Mom. "Want some?"

I wished I could say yes. "I gotta take care of something kind of urgent right now. Tomorrow?"

"Whatever," said Mom over her shoulder as she went into the kitchen, her gray dress moving under the soft lights like the sea when the wind passes over and the water ripples.

I headed to the bar.

Phil dropped the wet highball glass of iced pineapple juice on a cocktail napkin beside my fist. He skewered two cherries and a slick black olive with a toothpick. *Glunk.*

"A Claudeline special with all the bells and whistles. You've always had a sophisticated sensibility for a kid."

"I don't feel that way lately," I said.

"Life experience. That's all you're missing, Claude. You still got lessons to learn out there."

"Phil, I gotta ask you about something important."

Behind Phil, Mom appeared in the big square window to the kitchen. When she saw me talking to Phil, she did a double take. "I thought you were leaving?"

"I am," I said. "In five minutes."

"Five minutes," said Mom in her *I mean it* voice.

I nodded, and she disappeared.

Phil looked over his shoulder at where Mom had been. "How a woman with a face like your mother's can curdle milk by the gallon with one look, it never made sense to me. Does it to you?"

I felt a little guilty, but I laughed.

"Learned a new word from my angel niece that describes your mother and me perfectly. *Frenemies.* It means friends plus enemies." Phil cackled.

"You're totally frenemies," I said.

Phil hauled a rack of clean glasses from one side of the bar to the other. "Anyways, Claude, what's up? You neighborhood punks need help working out a prank? Tell ya who'd be an easy target. That bodega on the corner by your place. Schlub works twenty-four hours a day. Sleep deprivation. I'd clean him out bit by bit till he ain't got nothin' left to hock but dog chow."

I'd stopped stealing from our bodega once I bought the green beans, but I didn't feel like getting into the concept of thinking about other people's feelings with Phil at the moment. No need to frighten the man.

"Not a prank, or whatever. It's the sick-girl scam," I said. "Alma Lingonberry."

"Who now?" said Phil.

"The sick girl, with the flyers everywhere?"

The wrinkles around Phil's eyes made starbursts. "Funny-lookin' kid?"

"That's the one," I said. "Have you heard anything about her? On the streets, I mean."

Phil shook his head slowly. "Kiddo, I'm too old to keep track of that kind of stuff."

"Well, if you had to guess. Who do you think's behind it?" I said.

"You lookin' for a cut or somethin'?" asked Phil, winking.

"Somethin' like that," I said.

Phil made his bottom lip puff out and looked above me, like the answer to my question was across the street.

That's when I remembered: There was a reason my grandfathers liked Phil's old tavern so much. Phil knew nothing.

"I get it Phil," I said. "If you see somethin'—"

Phil and I finished the sentence together: "Don't say nothin'!"

When Phil's cackling trailed off, he said, "Tell ya what, kiddo. I'll keep my ears open, all right? For you."

He reached for a bowl of bright yellow lemons and smiled a half smile that made me wonder, out of nowhere, if he was happy. Which made this the perfect opportunity to test out my new style of being a better listener.

"How are you feeling, Phil?" I asked.

"Tired of workin'," he said. "You know why people become bartenders, Claude, instead of doing something really intelligent?"

"Why?" I asked.

Phil grabbed a cutting board and a knife. "I was askin'."

I hopped off my stool. "I'll keep my ears open," I said. "For you."

When I got home, I texted Brett and Lala. *Mom's off the hook. Waiting for Dad.* Then I settled in on the green leather couch. Streetlights and a lonely tune from a distant saxophone seeped in through the windows. I listened for a while, then turned on the television and started flipping channels. I hit a rerun of *Law & Order* about a cop who went psycho, and I fell asleep.

In the middle of the night I noticed Dad beside me, watching a cooking channel with the volume low. I was covered in a blanket, and my sandals were off. I cuddled my head against his leg. He felt cozy, for a rat.

"Too loud?" whispered Dad.

"Hm-mh," I said, already back asleep.

When I caught myself, I bolted upright.

"Dad!" I yelled.

Dad jumped. "Nightmare?" He put his hand on my back.

"Dad," I said. I checked all his earrings, the silver hoops and balls and the black scorpion, and all his rings, the fish and the knots and the silver bands. He was my dad no matter what. He was here, and he was alive.

Dad waved his hand in front of my eyes. "Are you awake?"

While I'd been asleep, an idea had flown into my brain. It was flapping its wings and kicking my head like a rooster in a cockfight. I had to grab its leg before it flew away. But first, the truth.

"Father, I need you to be completely honest about something," I said.

Dad chuckled. "Father?"

I gave him my statue stare. "Why are you helping Alma Lingonberry? You do know the whole thing is a scam."

"You sound like Mom," said Dad. "Fine. You wanna talk about this?"

I threw my hands in the air. "Ya think?!"

Dad stretched his neck and cracked his knuckles. "Claude, you gotta understand. Growing up like your mother did, Sara doesn't trust nobody. But me? I remember when my ma was dying. It was *rough*. I am all for that stuff—making friends, lending hands, and what have you. For a while I was embarrassed. The guys gave me a hard time. Believe that. But you know what, *Daughter*? Lately, I feel good about me. See, I made changes. Me and the guys are gonna raise a few thousand more for that kid too. Mom can live her life paranoid if she needs to. Taking those things down as fast as I can put them back up. We're Heckle and Jeckle out there."

To be sure I was all the way awake, I pulled out an arm hair.

I yelped.

Unbelievable.

Only one question remained.

"Who are Heckle and Jeckle and what do they have to do with this?"

"Old-school cartoon," said Dad, smiling, with the teeth.

My parents weren't evil. They were just insane, like everybody else.

I sighed, like, four times.

Dad pointed at me. "See, I told your mom we should get you checked for asthma. That stupid expressway makes all the kids sick—"

"It's not asthma, Father. I am fried. And I got a favor to ask."

The idea, from my dream. I wasn't sure about the details yet, but (minus the dancing piranhas and the singing snowman) it felt like the next step.

"Name it, shorty," said Dad.

"I need an appointment ASAP with your man in the FBI. It ain't about Grandpa; I'll let you handle that."

"You *what*?" said Dad.

"A meeting," I said. "That's the next step."

I rubbed the inside of my ear and yawned loud as

I snuggled beside Dad's leg. Sleep was dragging me off again, and I had no desire to fight it.

Dad lowered his voice. "How do you know about the FBI, Claude? Seriously. Is it obvious?"

"Not at all, Simon," I mumbled. "And feel free to let me know if you have any other questions. But maybe make it tomorrow."

Dad chuckled. "Well, I'd rather introduce you to the FBI than have you bugging me about taking over Pop's business." He tucked my hair behind my ear. "The *next step*, huh? You know what Grandpa used to say about you? 'Claudeline walks a few steps ahead of the rest of us.'"

"Which means what?" I mumbled.

"It means you're smarter than we are." Dad patted my back. "He was right about that much."

Smart, I thought. *I'll take it.*

That's when sleep yanked me onto the last car of its train, right as the doors were closing.

GOTCHA!

Interviewer: *What kind of advice would
you give to young people today?*
Ágnes Heller, philosopher: *None.*
When I was young I hated it when old people gave me advice.

The next morning, the N train was crammed with passengers. They sat, stood, dangled, and got smashed into
smears against doors. Arms floated free from bodies.
Strangers practically slow-danced. On the benches, rear
ends were wedged so tightly together that when one
budged, the whole row went *pop!* If you dropped your
phone, you knew it was never coming back. I cradled
mine in my fist and texted Brett and Lala to give them
the update: *Dad's off the hook. Heading to FBI interview.*
Meet at Green-Wood Cemetery, 4PM.

Dad and I were sitting on top of each other, but he
was politely looking away to give me my phone privacy.
Normally, he took a car service to his meetings with his
Friend Downtown. That's the code I was using in public
for his FBI agent—I think I got it from a movie, maybe?

But I convinced him to ride the subway. I wanted to feel the whole city hugging me, propping me up, as I got closer to meeting the person who was taking down Grandpa's business. Even if it was the right thing to do, I still felt sad about it.

A rush-hour train also seemed like the best place to convince Dad that Alma Lingonberry was a fraud. There's nothing realer than being an ingredient in a massive human sandwich. I figured it'd help him *Snap out of it!*

"Baffled" is kinda like "scowling"—another word I've never heard anybody use in real life. But baffled is what Dad was when I told him the Alma story, from the beginning.

"So you were friends with her?" said Dad. "And she punked you?"

"And Lala," I said. "And Brett's mom, and you, and—"

"But so, okay," said Dad, who was using one hand to keep a large butt in purple stretch pants from nuzzling itself against his cheek. "And you know the kid is not real . . . how?"

He made me explain everything about fifty times. I lingered over the Ferris wheel part, broke down some Chinese philosophy, and threw in some stuff about hearing Grandpa's warbled voice from the grave, and how even though he was speaking Russian, I somehow understood every word, which was when Dad said, "I think I've heard enough, kid."

"So you believe me?" I asked.

The train whirred in the background. Dad shook his head. "You're saying your gut instinct tells you she's not real. Sara said the same thing—but she assumes everybody has something to hide. I don't know."

"You don't have to decide now," I said. "Let me explain everything to your Friend Downtown."

"Yeah, well, that dude is his own nonsense," said Dad.

"What dude? Your Friend Downtown?" I asked.

Dad nodded.

"What do you mean?"

"Forget it," said Dad, as he leaned his head back against the darkened subway window. "You're so far ahead of me, Claude, it's embarrassing."

"Are you kidding?" I said. "You're in the lead."

"Yeah?" he said.

"Of course," I said.

As soon as I said it, I knew it was true. Dad had some serious courage, ratting to the FBI. If I was feeling sad, he must've been feeling something way more complicated. I made a mental note to ask him about that later, when we weren't on public transportation.

When the train pulled into our stop, we did a mini fist bump (which was all we had room for), shimmied through the crowd, saying, "Excuse me, excuse me, thank you, excuse me," and leaped onto the platform.

"It's prob'ly a ten-minute walk from here," said Dad. "But I always get a black-and-white cookie from this guy on the corner first."

"Aw!" I said. "It's your treat for showing up, right?"

"Doesn't hurt," said Dad. "Want one?"

I hadn't expected to be so paranoid just from walking into an FBI office. Maybe it's in my blood. Everybody who looked me in the eye and sized me up, I looked her in the eye and sized her up. The security guards, the secretaries, the people walking down the hallways. One lady, the lady in charge of letting people into some room where you wait to get into some other room, stared at me so hard with her blue eyeliner and black eyeballs and I stared at her so hard with my nostrils twitching that a whole group of people in suits and white shirts stopped in front of us. One of them asked Dad, "Is everything all right here?" Which shocked the lady into being more appropriate, and so I won the staring contest and was satisfied. I gave the group my innocent girly smile. It's modeled on Lala's, but like the smile of a certain hostess we know and love, it Needs Improvement. A couple people smiled back, but they looked more suspicious, not less, so I switched back to my plain and regular face.

"We're waiting for Gotcha," said Dad.

A tall guy laughed. "Gotcha!" he said.

"Gotcha!" said the lady next to him. And they kept going down the carpeted hallway.

When they were far enough away, I whispered, "Do people around here seem shady to you?"

Dad patted my back. "You get used to it."

"What's with the 'gotcha' thing?" I asked.

Then a man with shoulders as wide as a sideways double-decker tour bus walked up to Dad and shined his teeth at him. I mean, he aimed his teeth at Dad and turned them on like a flashlight, and looked down, way down, at me. His voice was booming, like a microphone was hiding in his shirt collar and we were on the news, or the *Saturday Night Live* version of the news, where the reporters have half a brain and the news comes out as jokes.

"Claudeline Feng LeBernardin, born eleven years ago under an auspicious sign, heir to the Song family throne. Wow. I mean, *wow*."

A tan hand appeared in front of my face. I didn't shake it.

"Let's step into my office," said the man.

Dad followed him.

I didn't move. *You understand what I'm doing here, right, Grandpa?* I thought.

And as I stood there, I swore I heard him answer.

(In English, not Russian. And his voice wasn't warbly; it was normal.)

You're in charge now, Claudeline. Remember? I don't have to understand. You do.

Dad turned back. "You okay?"

I nodded and followed them.

The FBI guy escorted us down a hallway with paintings of deflated flowers on the walls, and into an office. He sat behind a heavy-looking metal desk and pulled out a pad of paper and a pen. Dad sat in a dull green chair. Another pad of paper and a box of crayons that had never been opened were stacked on a table beside a small rocking chair. Guessing that was my spot, I took a seat and rocked.

"Get many tweens in here, sir?" I asked, looking at the crayons.

"You're not the first, C-Feng." The FBI guy pressed his palms together and rested his fingertips on his lips. "What's the matter? Catch you off guard? Claudeline Feng LeBernardin, street name C-Feng. *Gotcha!*"

I looked at Dad. He shook his head.

"So Simon," said the FBI guy. "No Sara today?"

"No dice," said Dad.

The FBI guy studied his fingers like they were a word search he'd half quit working on. "C-Feng, C-Feng. Your mother is the ancient walled land whose gates admit neither friend nor foe. What mortal can penetrate those sphinxian guards?"

"In English, Hank," said Dad.

The FBI guy spun his chair to gaze out his window. "Your Sara is a tough cookie." His chair kept spinning until it faced us again. "Anyway, cats, you've got new information for me? A line on some illegal weapons, C-Feng? Black market? Money laundering? We've touched on a lot already, but whatever you can add will be a heap of help for my ongoing below-the-radar, barely funded investigation into the gangs of Sunset Park."

"May I ask your name, sir?" I said.

The FBI guy snapped a card out of his jacket in one flick, like he'd been practicing at home in the mirror. "Federal Agent Hank Banazio. But just like you, C-Feng, the fellas call me by my street name."

"Let me guess," I said.

All at once, now: Federal Agent Hank Banazio, Dad, and I said, *"Gotcha!"*

Banazio (I refuse to use his "street name") made me wonder if we'd regret including the FBI in our plan. But instead of worrying, I took the next step. On his desk I spread out a few Alma flyers I'd collected from the neighborhood that morning.

"There's a girl," I said. "Or should I say, somebody pretending to be a girl."

Banazio leaned over the flyers. "What's this? Some twisted poetry cult?"

"Alma here is taking donations," I said.

Banazio held a flyer to the light, like he was inspecting it for fingerprints or a secret code. "Mmmm-hm," he said.

Was Banazio insane? I snuck a look at Dad, but he didn't notice. He was spaced out, like he was prepared to spend a few hours being totally bored.

Finally Banazio asked, "So, C-Feng, what's the plan?"

I checked Dad again—still absent. So I said, "Well, I was thinking we could get whoever's being Alma to show up someplace. To, like, take a donation? And you could spy on her from behind the curtain, or something. And catch her in the act!"

Banazio clapped and pumped his fist in the air, as giddy as one of those disco roller skaters in Central Park. "I haven't seen potential for a *Gotcha!* moment like this one in years!"

"Really?" I said.

Dad seemed to be tuning back in. "Hold up, Hank."

"Give me a date, a time, and an address, and with the USA as my witness, I'll be there to take credit for your hard work," said Banazio.

"You don't wanna know the plan?" I said.

Banazio stood. "The less I know, the better I feel. Delegating is the key to managerial success."

"Hold up!" said Dad.

Banazio picked up a duffel bag. "Let's do it again tomorrow, Simon. I'm off to the gym. Tell Sara howdy-do. See you when I slap on the cuffs, C-Feng!"

Dad was totally awake now. "Hank—no! I don't want my kid busting some criminal!"

I stood. "Oh, come on, Dad. You have no idea where I am, ever. For all you know I spend every day at the Port Authority bus station screaming 'America the Beautiful' at the top of my lungs."

Dad flared his nostrils at me. "You are not doing this all by yourself. You are eleven years old."

"So you're both in!" Banazio gripped Dad's shoulder. "Si, gimme a buzz with the deets ASAP. Let's lock up the Brooklyn bard before she beatboxes the borough into oblivion."

"We'll call you!" I said, as I stuck out my hand for a shake. Banazio's hand was warmer and gentler than I'd imagined it would be.

"What just happened?" said Dad.

"I never miss an opportunity to play ball in Chinatown," said Banazio in a dreamy voice, on his way out the door. "Claudeline LeBernardin, welcome to the FBI."

Dad scooted inside the taxi beside me and slammed the door. Our driver was having a phone conversation that required extreme yelling in a thick Irish accent. As soon as Dad told her where we were going, we shot into traffic and she went back to yelling. I was pretty sure she had too much on her mind to be driving, let alone eaves-dropping, so I turned to Dad.

"I love that corny fed!" I said. "Where'd you find him?"

Dad rubbed his face like he was waking himself up. "Everybody on Eighth Avenue knows Gotcha. He's always hanging around, trying to get people to talk to him and give him information about crimes or what-ever."

"I didn't know him," I said.

"Your mom and I aren't perfect parents, but we get some things right."

"If you don't like Banazio," I said, "why are you rat-ting to him? Or whatever the nice word for that is."

Dad drummed his knees with his fingertips. He really did have a talent for looking comfortable and uncomfortable at the same time. Maybe he was com-fortable being uncomfortable. Or uncomfortable being comfortable.

Finally he said, "Like everybody says, Claude, I'm not like Grandpa."

I felt in my pocket for the creased-up, worn-out photograph I'd been carrying around all summer. As our taxi wove through Manhattan, Dad and I looked at it, together. Grandpa's hair was still black, and Dad was positively a butterball.

"This was on your wall, right?" said Dad. "From the

trip we took after my mother died." He looked more closely. "You know Grandpa traveled half the world on foot, on buses, even on a *raft* to get to New York City? It nearly killed him. Cost a ton too. He told me that every time he turned over the cash he earned sweating in some terrible job to pay the people who brought him to the United States, he swore he'd figure out how to get on the other side of that transaction. Someday people would hand cash to *him*, you know?"

"Why didn't he just open a store?" I asked.

"You say 'just,'" said Dad, "like it's so easy. But him, yeah. Pop could've done anything."

I thought about all those nights at the Wharfman's Shore, Grandpa shouting to the whole tavern how he was gonna leave everything to me instead of Dad.

"Grandpa used to try to make you depressed that you weren't as tough as him, didn't he?" I asked.

"My dad was tough in one way. Tough isn't really my thing. You, though, you're as tough as Grandpa," said Dad. "It's what you wanna do with it."

I noticed that Dad's eyes were sort of the same color as Sixtieth Street. An easy color, like walking home.

"BQE ain't movin'," said the taxi driver. "We'll cut through downtown."

The rain started again, in smacks and splats. It sounded like a radio station coming into tune.

When Dad leaned forward, his hair fell over his face.

"Now you and me gotta clarify some stuff. And listen to me, too, because I am your father."

"Stop using your CDs as Frisbees?" I said.

"No." Dad adjusted his earrings and rings. Then he looked me right in the eye and said, "I am your plan."

"What's that supposed to mean?" I asked.

"Meaning," said Dad, "if you really can get this Alma girl—this whoever—to show up someplace, I'm the one who's gonna be in the room with her. Or with him, or with them. Not you."

"What?" I said.

Dad took my chin. "Listen to me. I don't know why you're all Sherlock Holmes on this thing, but it sounds positive, and I'm proud of you, so I'm gonna back you up. But I won't put you in the same room with another thug. That's something I promised myself. I wanna be a better parent to you, Claude. And so, make some kind of plan, and tell me what you come up with. If I'm cool with it, it's gonna be me in there, doing it. That's my rule."

When Dad let go of my chin, he looked extra uncomfortable, but I knew he was right. The real Alma might be dangerous. Dad was looking out for me. That was when another idea poked its head through the smoke-colored day, swooped through the taxicab window, and landed, fully formed, on my shoulder. I rested my head against Dad's arm and smiled.

"You got it, Dad," I said.

His voice cracked, like I'd caught him off guard. "Really?"

"Mm-hm," I said. "We'll be in a different room."

"Who is we?" asked Dad.

"Don't worry about it," I said. "So, hey. This Banazio guy ain't a mental case?"

"Oh, he *is*." Dad motioned with his hands like he was smoothing a tablecloth. "Totally."

He had to be. Banazio was gonna let us set up Alma ourselves, instead of opening a file on her, dumping it in a bucket, and forgetting about it.

Perfect.

A JOURNEY OF A KAZILLION MILES

It's one world, pal. We're all neighbors.
—Frank Sinatra

Green-Wood Cemetery is bigger than the park, and quieter, since people are not there for fun. Brett, Lala, and I wound our way through its stretched-out hills while the wind and the trees had a conversation, the wind blowing their branches one way, the trees whipping them back. When we got to my grandfather's grave, a light sprinkling of rain joined in, letting the wind blow it, and the trees catch it and drop it again, until it settled in the grass and sank into the dirt.

We sat cross-legged on the ground. Dampness soaked through my jeans. It made me feel connected to the spot where Grandpa Si was turning from a living person into a memory.

Brett and Lala never asked why we were meeting at

the cemetery where my grandfather is buried. I wasn't sure what I would've told them, if they had. It was almost like they knew, or they didn't know but it didn't matter. It was amazing to me that even with friends like each other, we'd gotten suckered by Alma. She kind of *was* a sniper.

I told them about my meeting with Banazio and explained the idea I'd had in the taxicab about how we could set up Alma. While I talked, the fluttering leaves on the trees sounded like clapping. I felt like Grandpa Si was with us, cheering us on. Like he was the wind shaking the branches so the truth could fly out and cover the sky with exclamation points. Whether Grandpa's help would've been a good thing or a bad thing, I couldn't tell you. But I liked to think he'd want to help, even if it was just a wish, or a dream.

"Jeez, Claude, you got a lot farther with this than I did," said Brett. "All I learned is that lingonberries grow wild in the forests of Scandinavia. Apparently, they make great jam."

"Kelvin told me Alma's e-mails are untraceable without, like, a warrant," said Lala. "But that's all I got. I love your idea!"

Brett nodded. "If we can pull it off, it'll be *classic*."

We all agreed on the next step: I needed to have a chat with a certain television producer. While I tried to track down her number, I overheard Brett and Lala analyzing Money's fear of leaving his house. Money may not have been the least shady friend a kid could dig up, but talking about him was sort of like our hobby.

I don't know if normally over in television land they get a bunch of kooks making crank calls asking to speak to Kermit the Frog or what, but it took half an hour for me even to get to Rita's assistant's assistant, who asked me a pile of trick questions, such as "You say that you are acquainted with Ms. Flannigan via *whom*?" and "Did you want to put your mother on the phone?"

I suppose it didn't help that I didn't know Rita's last name was Flannigan and not "The Producer." I mean, why would I?

Finally: "Margarita Flannigan's office," said Rita's actual assistant; then I got put on hold for another ten thousand minutes.

And then: "Claudeline! What a treat to hear from you!"

Rita's phone voice sounded jolly and confident. I could almost see her sitting at a glass desk with her legs crossed on top, and several security guards who had been alerted to a random phone call from a possible psycho leaning over her with their earphones plugged into our conversation.

"Can you please give me your cell phone number, for future reference?" I asked.

Then I explained our plan to bust Alma, and how

Rita could help us. At first she was skeptical. Then she had a ton of questions. Then she sounded nervous. And then she sounded confident again.

Too confident.

"Your plan is adorable," said Rita, "but you'll have to find someone else to help you with it."

Adorable. I suspected she'd say something like that. Rita's confident voice could not cover the fact that she was a total scaredy-cat.

I paced between graves. Fake flowers glowing neon bright shimmered in the breeze.

"We need you, Rita," I said. "You, specifically. Because you're the only legit rich person I know."

"Crimes and setups and the FBI and this type of thing? It's normal for you, Claude," said Rita. "But it's not my world! My father was—"

"If it's not your world, why are you writing a screenplay about it?" I said.

There was a pause.

"I told you I shouldn't write a screenplay about your family!" said Rita.

I paced the other direction. "Wrong answer, Rita. Wrong. The right answer is that everybody lives in the same, messed-up world. And since you and me met, we're even more in each other's worlds. The question is, can you do something now that might make a difference, or are you gonna stay stuck on the same barstool, in the same city, having the same depressing life forever?"

There was another pause.

"Ouch," said Rita.

"You can put that whole thing in your screenplay," I said.

"Oh, Claude," said Rita. "I don't know about making a difference in the world. But I do, do, do want to finish my screenplay. Sheesh. Helping you *would* give me the opportunity to polish up my gangster dialogue. And I did meet lots of characters at the carnival. Oh, I shouldn't. I shouldn't . . ."

I got Brett and Lala's attention, gave them a thumbs-up and mouthed, *She's in.*

I'll tell you right now I'm not gonna describe every eensy-weensy detail of every baby ant that stomped through every muddy footprint of the rest of the steps of our plan to take out Alma. I'm not trying to bore my own face off.

So let me put it like this. When I hung up with Rita, we all walked back to Sixtieth Street. I left Brett and Lala at Brett's place and ran home to talk to Dad, since, as he put it, he *was the plan*, and I needed to make sure he was down with it.

I found Dad sitting in the kitchen with his feet crossed on top of the table, eating microwave popcorn from the bag. He kept saying stuff that sounded like philosophy to me, such as "There is no reason that any of this should be happening" and "My life went from tragic to ridiculous in a hot second" and "Watching television all summer will give a kid some wack ideas. I shoulda enrolled you in soccer, or whatever, right?"

But the important thing was, Dad was in.

The only person left to convince was Alma.

When I got back to Brett's, the front door was propped open, and I heard Mother Fingerless yelling.

"Fine! Abandon your mother!"

"Ma, don't you think you're exaggerating, slightly?"

"That sweet lady with the music-video hair. She'll help me."

I went into the kitchen. Brett was holding the back of a chair at arm's length, like he needed it to keep from falling over. He shook his head. Lala was sitting at the table, eating a bowl of soup, trying to make herself look extra small. Mother Fingerless was standing beside her, holding a big brown vase full of red plastic roses with one hand. With the other she scrubbed the table underneath it hard and fast.

Mother Fingerless looked up. "Claudeline! You know about computers. You're coming to the library with me. We raise two hundred dollars at the carnival, for *charity*, and my son tells me, 'Ma, you gotta keep it'?" She crumpled her paper towel and stomped around, like she'd forgotten where she kept the trash can. "I should've been firmer with you, Brett. When you told me you were finished with church, I thought, 'Okay. Better to let him fly back when he needs comfort and education than force him to stay.' But you know what? I was wrong. Claudeline, let's go."

Mother Fingerless slammed the vase on the table and left the room with her crumpled-up paper towel. The vase fell on its side.

"Let's go!" she yelled, from the hallway to the front door.

Brett stood up straight and pulled his curls.

"She doesn't believe us about Alma," said Lala.

"I can see that," I said.

"Claudeline!" yelled Mother Fingerless.

"She's busy, Ma!" yelled Brett. "Give her a break!"

I heard Mother Fingerless knocking around like she was gathering her things to leave. "Fine. The lady with the rock-and-roll hair. She's respectful . . ."

The door slammed.

"She's processing," said Brett.

Lala went to the sink to rinse out her bowl. "Whoever is putting your moms through this needs to get taken *out*," she said. Then we all headed back to my place to invite Alma to our party. Technically that party would be a funeral for a girl who didn't exist, but we were calling it a celebration of her life.

My legs dangled over the edge of my bed, and my sandals dangled off my toes. Lala was on my right, lying on her belly with her head propped on her fists. Brett was on my left, sitting cross-legged. My curtains were closed so we could all see the computer screen.

To: Lil.Poet123@xmail.com
From: ClaudelineLeBernardin5@xmail.com

Dear Alma,

Sorry I haven't written since the carnival. How was your emergency treatment? Even though I have not written, I have been thinking of you.

Especially, I have been thinking about how hard it is for you to pay for all those treatments. That has really been bothering me. So I would like to solve your problem, once and for all.

My family is in a highly profitable business, as I mentioned to you before. And we know people. People who can make things look good on paper.

"I feel like we're in a spy movie right now, Claude," said Lala, wiggling around.

"Awesome," said Brett, shaking his head.

I'm gonna be straight with you, Alma. We know a television producer. She wants to buy your life story. She can offer you as much money as you need, beginning with a check for ten thousand dollars.

No questions asked.

Naturally, we will take a small to medium percentage of the proceeds in exchange for making these arrangements. Of course, getting well is more important than money. But sometimes money makes you feel better. Much better, even.

If it works out? You never know. Maybe we can keep doing business together. We're always looking for new partners.

This is a limited-time offer. We can meet you in person, this Sunday, at noon. If you're interested, call me for the details. Sending e-mails sprayed with perfume might work for small businesses like yours. We prefer to look people in the eye.

I understand if you want to avoid my family. Most people do. What can I say? This kind of thing is in my blood. At least, I had to make the offer. I always take care of my friends.

Love your very best pal in the whole wide world

"That's a bit much," said Brett, pointing at the word "love."

I deleted the last line.

Yours truly,
Friend #206
Claude

I added my phone number, sent the e-mail, and shut my laptop. I could tell you that I felt woozy, or drunk on power, or had an urge to do the electric slide, but the truth is, I felt normal. Like what I was doing had a destiny of its own, and I'd be smart not to get in its way.

"In the movies," said Brett, "this is the part where we say, 'Now, we wait.'"

Lala giggled. "Now," she said, "we—"

But she couldn't finish her sentence, because my phone rang.

THE PHONE CALL

When we are near, we must make the enemy believe we are far away; when far away, we must make him believe we are near.
—Sun Tzu, philosopher

Nobody ever calls me. Nobody. *Ever.* The few times I've heard my ringtone, which is the theme music from an old-timey horror movie called *Psycho*, which Brett and I chose after listening to about a hundred options, my first thought was, *Somebody needs to answer that.* It rang twice before Lala grabbed the phone and shoved it at my ear.

"Hello?" I said.

Brett and Lala pressed their ears to the phone.

"Claude?" whispered a husky voice.

Lala gripped my arm. I felt Brett stop breathing.

I said, "Is this—"

The voice had a loud coughing fit, so loud I had to lean away. Brett frowned. Lala scrunched her nose. Finally, the voice whispered, "It's Alma. Can't talk."

"I can barely hear you," I said. "Can you—"

The voice interrupted. "Can we do this over PayPal?"

Now *I* stopped breathing. Brett, Lala, and me all looked at each other.

And we were all thinking the same thing.

Since the carnival, we'd known in our hearts that Alma was a fraud. But we knew it in the way you know the North Pole exists, and polar bears live there, building igloos. Which they don't—build igloos, I mean. What I'm saying is, we knew Alma didn't exist, but we weren't clear on the details. Now we had a voice on the phone asking us to send cash. Was it a man or a woman? A boy or a girl? I couldn't tell, and it didn't matter.

Alma wasn't real, but our situation had never been realer. The voice on the phone was asking us to send cash. Cash it knew for a fact was dirty.

The voice on the phone was a criminal.

Something inside me sat up, put on a fresh coat of lipstick and straightened its bow tie.

Unfortunately for Alma Lingonberry, criminals were my comfort zone.

Lala and Brett had to lean away slightly as I wiggled my fingers into the pocket of my black jean skirt. I balanced my photograph on my knees. Grandpa Si's eyes glimmered.

Whaddaya think, Grandpa? I thought.

You've set the wheels in motion, Claude, said Grandpa. *Let's get the sick girl on board and roll.*

I cleared my throat. Not because there was anything

stuck in it—it just felt like the thing to do.

"No offense, Alma Lingonberry," I said, "but online transactions are an amateur's game." Lala and Brett leaned back in to the phone. "You want the cash, you gotta meet with my family, and our television producer, in person. And we want this to look legit, so you better rustle up a legal guardian, too."

There was a pause. Then the voice whispered, "Okay. So where do we do this?"

Lala made an *Eee!* face at Brett and me.

I started to tell her. "Come to—"

Brett shook his finger to interrupt. He mouthed, *Let's send a car to pick her up.*

I nodded. "Give us an address, Alma. Our people will pick you up."

There was a pause. For a few seconds, I couldn't hear anything.

Then the voice said, "The clock tower."

Lala leaned away and mouthed, *Not the hospital?* She did a massive eye roll.

I couldn't resist asking. "You won't have any problem getting out of the hospital, then?"

There was another pause.

"This sounds like a swell adventure," said the voice. Then it hung up.

Lala jumped up and stomped across my bed in her

yellow dress. She looked like a baby chick on springs. "This! Is! Happening!"

Brett put his hand on my shoulder. "Well done, Claude. Couldn't have gone smoother."

This was one of the many times since I'd met Brett that I would've given anything to be able to crawl into his deep brown eyes and take a nap. Unfortunately, it wasn't time to rest yet. Instead, I sighed, Brett squeezed my shoulder, and we all reviewed the plan for Sunday. When he and Lala went home, I tossed my phone on my pillow, but the scruffy voice lingered in my ear.

I put my photograph on my desk and took a seat. As far as I was concerned, the Tale of Alma Lingonberry and her Circle of Ten Thousand Friends couldn't have been over soon enough.

But endings are not easy. They make everything that already happened look different, like it was all leading up to that. And once you've got your ending, it's time to start something new.

I'll never know why my grandfather became a gangster. What he went through on the raft to New York City, or in the terrible jobs, or the exact shape of every hole he left behind.

Maybe it was like what Brett said about his father. Sometimes people take a wrong turn in life and never figure out a way back. Now it was up to me to try to make it to the happy ending Grandpa was walking toward, all along.

You don't have to love everything a person does to love the person. After all, you don't know what it's like to be someone else unless you have been there.

On the other hand, use your imagination. That's what it's there for.

THE SUNSET PARK CREW AND THE BUST OF THE CENTURY

Never give a sword to a man who can't dance.
—Unknown

The Sunday of the bust, Mother Fingerless was sitting on an easy chair with her feet up, watching a television show with dramatic music. When Brett called, "Bye, Ma," she said, *"Hmph!"* It was obvious from the way she'd quit asking to send money that she finally believed us about Alma. But she wasn't quite ready to admit that yet, so she was pouting.

"Why aren't you at church?" I asked. "Devil getcha?"

"You scamp," she said. "I hurt my foot."

"I'm gonna make your rascal son here bring you back some takeout, okay?"

"I'm not hungry," she said, sounding like she was a little kid.

"Well then, we'll bring you some ice cream," I said. "Ice cream's good when you're not hungry."

"Hmph," said Mother Fingerless. "I like the black sesame flavor they got at the place on Eighth Avenue."

"Got it," said Brett, and we blew her some kisses and headed out the door.

We spotted Laliyah on the corner of Eighth Avenue and Sixtieth Street. She was decked out in a ruffled peach skirt and a shiny yellow T-shirt. Silver ribbons wove their way through her braids and shimmered in the brightness as the seconds ticked closer to high noon. That's what they call it in westerns. When the sun lets nothing hide.

"You guys look smooth," said Lala.

I was wearing my green sundress with my gold heart necklace. Brett was in black jeans and a short-sleeve black button-down I'd never seen before. We all looked very professional.

"Thanks," said Brett. "What did you tell your mother?"

"Brunch with Andrew," said Lala. "Noodles count as brunch, right?" She handed me a pile of greeting cards.

"Um . . . ?" I said.

"So I'm at the drugstore, doing my nails," said Lala. "And Kelvin's birthday is coming up. I'm like, yeah, lemme check these out. Open one."

The top card on the pile had a picture of a laughing baby. Inside, it said:

How precious life seems

When you're following

Your dreams

"Okay . . . ?" I said.

"No?" said Lala. "Do the next one."

A glittering green tree on a creamy background.

For a girl

Who's like a tree

I'm glad to be

Your friend.

"Wait," I said. "That's almost the same as my Alma poem."

"They're *all* Alma poems," said Lala. "She pretty much stayed in this section called General Inspiration. It's between Happy Anniversary and Get Well Soon."

So I could've bought the poem that touched my heart at the drugstore for a dollar ninety-nine. Good to know.

"I can't wait to send Alma our condolences," said Brett.

"Right?" said Lala, taking the cap off a purple marker. "I'm about to sign all these. 'Dear Alma. Go ahead and bite my style next. See what happens.'"

"Nobody could bite your style, Lala," said Brett. "You're completely original."

That was true. No matter how much you might pretend to be somebody else, you can't fake the person you really are. The truth is out there in the shadows, waiting to tell the world the rest of the story.

We all jumped different directions to avoid Money's speeding scooter. He crashed into the street sign. "Sorry, kids," he said, dusting himself off.

"Don't text and scoot," said Brett. "You'll impale somebody."

"Gotta keep in touch with my Scott Jones friends. Just because you guys forced me to leave the office doesn't mean I ain't still workin'. Though I admit I'm looking forward to shaking Alma's hand. She's my guiding light."

"Remind me, please, why I like you?" said Lala.

"Because I'm bad news," said Money.

Lala looked him up and down. "Yeah, you're a real threat."

Money waggled his eyebrows and shoved his phone in the back pocket of his khakis, and we all headed up Eighth Avenue.

The spicy scent of the noodle shop made me glad we were meeting Alma on our home turf. Customers filled most of the tables, except for the one Mr. Chin had marked with a paper tent that said RESERVED.

"Hey, y'all," said Dad, knocking on the counter beside the cash register. He wore his usual leather vest and jewelry, but he had added a cheerful blue stripe to his hair. I kissed him, right on his scar. He fist-bumped Lala and Brett and pointed at Money. "Who's this kid?"

"I'm one of them!" said Money, sounding hurt.

"Sorry," said Dad. "I just never see you out with these guys."

"He's an indoor kid," said Lala, patting Money's back.

"Time for places?" asked Brett.

Mr. Chin led Brett, Lala, and Money through the kitchen.

Dad was giving off the comfortable-uncomfortable vibe.

"Having second thoughts, Dad?" I asked. "I'd be happy to trade places with you."

"No way," said Dad. "When I said I didn't want you in the room with whoever shows up today, I meant anywhere in the vicinity. You guys shouldn't even be on this block."

I didn't need him getting to the next stop on that train of thought.

"Love the stripe!" I said. "It brings out your eyes."

Dad smoothed his hair. "My stylist is amazing."

"Claude!" called Rita as she waltzed into the noodle

shop in a red pantsuit, swinging her shoulder bag and waving with two fingers at Mr. Chin like she was a regular.

"Ready to meet some new characters, Rita?" I said.

"I couldn't be less ready, Claudeline," said Rita. "But sometimes you get an offer you can't refuse. Get it? That's a line from one of those famous gangster movies. 'Make him an offer he can't refuse.' That also happens to be *exactly* what I plan to do to Alma Lingonberry."

Dad and I looked at each other.

"Um, Rita?" I said. "You do know that 'Make him an offer he can't refuse' means 'threaten to kill him.' Right?"

Rita's jaw fell halfway to her knees. She clutched her pearl necklace. *"Nooo."*

Dad folded his arms and puckered his lips like he was about to whistle.

Then Rita shook off her suit jacket, plopped her bag on the floor, and pulled out a leather folder. "Just playin' with ya. I'm down. Where is this Alma knucklehead?" She shook the folder. "I'm ready with the contract. The *offer*, that is."

Dad covered his mouth and laughed. He stuck out his hand to Rita, who shook it. "I'm Claude's pop."

"Margarita Flannigan," said Rita. "Let's do this."

Through the one-way mirror Brett, Lala, Money, and I could observe the whole noodle shop, crystal clear. The red-and-cream checkerboard tile, the sprinkling of square tables with napkin boxes, the yellow counter with the cash register, the lanterns hanging from the ceiling. The same view that was being transmitted via Mr. Chin's hidden cameras to his living room on Eleventh Avenue, where we'd sent Federal Agent Hank "Gotcha!" Banazio to watch the bust go down.

At first I'd figured Banazio would be with us, behind the one-way mirror. But as soon as I'd explained that part of the plan to Dad, he'd ruled it out. "Pop always told me to keep guys like Hank at a distance. He's got power, but he's unpredictable. Let him watch from Skippy's house and send over his cops to arrest whoever shows up. If he feels the need to take a bow, by the time he gets to the noodle shop it'll be too late for him to screw anything up." So we'd given Banazio the date, the time, and the address, like he'd asked for, without even telling him whose house it was. Mrs. Chin had agreed to be there to let him in and point him toward the TV screen.

Mr. Chin set a pot of hot tea, some cups, and a bowl of potato chips on a turned-over crate.

"Remember," he said, "you can hear us, but we can't hear you. I'll be taking customers as usual."

"Wonder where *Alma* is now?" said Lala.

"Doubt she'll flake with ten grand at stake," said Brett.

Money clutched his heart. "*Ten grand?* Scott Jones and I are about to take a turn for the worse!"

Brett and I both started to say something and stopped. The way Lala was staring at Money, she looked exactly like Mrs. Ramirez. We knew she'd deal with *Andrew* later.

While we waited for the guest of honor, Lala sucked us into a conversation about which of our teachers we should nominate for this television show where you get a free head-to-toe makeover if you throw away all your clothes. We had it narrowed down to five candidates when the black town car pulled in front of the restaurant.

"Agim!" I said.

Lala pressed her nose against the one-way mirror. *"AGIM!"*

Money jumped up. "Who's Agim, and what's so great about him?"

Brett looked over Money's shoulder. "Agim is the man with the car."

My heartbeat felt like thunder in my rib cage as we watched Agim get out of the At Your Service Car Service town car, pop the trunk, and pull out a folded-up wheelchair. When he opened the car's back door, Lala and I squeezed hands.

Then a man stepped out of the car and adjusted his cuff links.

I immediately assumed I was confused. But no. There was the wheelchair, and that was definitely Agim.

"Claudeline," said Brett. "That's Phil."

In slow motion, words arranged themselves into sentences inside my skull. *That's Phil. Phil is here. Here, at the noodle shop. Agim brought him.*

"Who's Phil?" asked Money.

"Claude?" said Lala. "Who's Phil?"

My heartbeat stepped on the gas. Blood rushed into my ears and made the room spin.

Agim brought Phil to the noodle shop. It's not a coincidence.

When I tried to breathe, my lungs shivered.

What is going on?

Brett put his hand on my back and talked fast. "Okay. So, okay. It's okay, Claude . . ." But his voice told me he knew how okay it was not.

I heard myself mumble, "Phil is Alma Lingonberry."

Brett tried to make a reassuring facial expression, but he ended up crinkling his forehead in a way that said, *I'm sorry.*

For the second time in my life the walls of the world I knew crumbled. What would happen if I leaned backward? Would I lean right through Brett's hand, and through the floor, and fall into a new universe, where this situation suddenly made sense?

And who had that been on the phone, when we'd set up the bust? Not Phil—his voice was unmistakable.

"Alma," said Lala quietly.

I refocused my eyes on the town car. A female with a long braid dangling over one shoulder was ducking out of it. She was crouching, but she was on the tall side. You wouldn't call her a *girl*. Agim helped her into the wheelchair.

Last out of the car was a guy in a dark suit who could've been Phil's twin, except for his hair, which was so black and shiny you could almost see the sky reflecting off it.

"The no-good brother-in-law," I said.

"Whose brother-in-law, Claude?" asked Brett, who was now gently holding my arm. "Phil's?"

I said, "Which makes Alma Phil's angel niece."

I couldn't believe I'd never asked her name.

Then, like the smell of rotting garbage on a hundred-degree day, the truth smacked me in the face so hard it almost broke my nose. *Phil has been e-mailing me, pretending to be a dying kid.* It took every scrap of je ne sais quoi I had not to put my fist through the one-way mirror, dive through the broken glass, and tackle him.

Brett took off his glasses and squinted. "Is that a spider's web?"

We all squinted. The no-good brother-in-law was tucking a blanket over Alma's lap. A tattoo of a spider's web crept up Alma's right cheek. They'd tried to mask it with a thick layer of orange powder.

That's when my ancient gangster instincts kicked in. Call 'em family values, if you will. Hundreds of years of history, in New York City, and China, and Corsica, and the caves where we learned to stand up straight, and the oceans where we swam before we grew arms and legs, and where, instead of worrying about the next thing that was gonna go wrong, or what it all meant, anyway, we darted through the sea with our eyes glued open, blowing bubbles.

As much as I wanted to chuck a wok of noodle soup at Phil's kneecaps, I wasn't gonna let that guy walk outta this situation with no bigger problems than a hairline fracture and a laundry bill.

The Thing was near. It was time to starve it.

I turned to Brett. "Everybody has to play along."

Brett nodded fast, like he'd been thinking the same thing. "The plan can still work, you know?"

I did know. Our bust could still work, even if the Alma we were busting was Phil.

It had to.

And he'd already made his first mistake. Phil was so concerned about increasing his profits, he hadn't been observing me carefully. He assumed I wouldn't rat on him for ripping people off. He'd get his cut, we'd get our cut, Rita would get whatever she got for working with the gang, and everybody'd walk away happy.

I concentrated on morphing my brain waves into radio waves broadcasting the message everybody needed to hear: *Play along.*

When Phil and the brother-in-law pushed Alma's wheelchair into the noodle shop, Dad was sitting at the RESERVED table, typing on his phone. Rita was sitting beside him, digging in her purse. At the same time, they looked up, saw Phil, and froze. Phil was expecting Dad and Rita, but Dad and Rita sure weren't expecting Phil.

Phil nodded. Dad stared. Rita blinked and fluffed her hair.

Play along, guys. Play along.

Phil checked out Mr. Chin, and the customers slurping noodles. "Where's Claude?" he asked.

Lala elbowed me.

"She's not here, Phil," said Dad, slowly standing. "She's a kid."

Come on, Dad, I thought. *Play along . . .*

But Rita got my brain-radio-wave message first. She stood and sang, *"Phiiil!"* drawing it out like she hadn't seen him in a year. "What a shock to find you in this . . . position! But then, I'm not one to ask questions, am I?"

Phil's face was more hawklike than ever. "Rita," he said in a flat voice. It was obvious he was feeling her out.

The no-good brother-in-law stuck out his hand to Rita for a shake and said, "It's Roger." I tried to place Roger, but I was pretty sure I'd never seen him before. Maybe him and the angel niece really did live in New Jersey.

Rita shook Roger's hand and smiled in a dazed way, like a toothpaste model. *This would be the moment for you to bust out that gangster dialogue, Rita,* I thought, but it looked like her face had gotten stuck. Rita stayed as glazed over as a Macy's mannequin.

Roger took a seat, leaned back, and crossed his legs. Phil took a seat beside him.

Dad just stared at them.

I was starting to feel desperate. "You can do it, Dad!" I said. "Play along!"

And then a voice inside Rita's head must've yelled, *Snap out of it!*

She clapped. "Anybody need an espresso? Make mine a double today, Skippy."

Phil nodded toward Mr. Chin. "You know this guy?"

"Of course! This is my spot!" Rita winked at Phil. "Well, my other spot."

Mr. Chin held up a finger. He wasn't helping a customer, but he didn't have an espresso machine, so I guessed he was stalling.

Then Rita faced the wheelchair and clasped her hands like when she opened them, a butterfly might escape to the ceiling. At this point I didn't see why it wouldn't. "And this must be our Alma!"

Alma threw up a mangled-looking gang sign and belched. "What up, dog?"

Lala gasped.

Rita peered deep into Alma's eyes, like she was the only person in the room who mattered. "My name is Rita Flannigan, and I am a television producer. As I'm sure your father told you, I'd be honored to turn your life story into a heartwarming dramatic series."

Alma cracked her gum loudly. "Make me a friggin' superstar."

"That's the idea!" said Rita.

As she sat back down, I noticed her eyebrows do a quick flinching thing I'd seen before, when I told her tall tales at Guillaume's. I guessed she was thinking something along the lines of *I can't put somebody like her in my screenplay. Nobody'd believe it!*

"What can I tell ya, Rita," I muttered. "Once in a while, this city deals you a doozy."

"What happens now, Si?" said Phil. "We get the cash and walk away here, or what?"

Dad sat down and scratched his scar, like he was making a decision about something. He stole a look at the hidden cameras that were transmitting all this into Mr. Chin's living room. Then he leaned back and let the blue streak fall over one of his eyes. "If you're down to pretend this chick is sick, and you're ready to put ink on some paperwork?" He stuck out his hand for a shake. "We got your money, man."

Phil's lips cracked slightly, enough for a half smile to leak out, as he leaned forward and shook Dad's hand.

Rita pulled the fake television contract out of the leather folder and cooed at Phil in a best-friends type of way. "Who's happier to be making a little extra cash these days, Philip? You or me?"

"Hard to say," he said. "I admit, when Claude told

me she had a television producer, it caught me off guard. I mean, you? Tangled up with the family business? But hey."

"We shouldn't be so surprised," said Rita. "You and me and Claudeline have always been in sync. It's like, excuse me, but if you think this country was built by idealists, you don't know your history." She raised her eyebrows.

Phil leaned forward and spoke quietly. "That's just it, Rita. People don't know. They don't care. Who do you think made this country great? Hippies ridin' bicycles?"

Rita opened a gold case that was about the right size to have a pen inside. "It's a free country! Make some money! Be *creative* for the love of—okay, I'm going off-topic . . ."

Had Phil's laughter always had such a screechy burn to it, like a car that takes a corner too fast and skids out of control?

"I'm sorry!" said Rita. "But Phil—you know? Roger? Right?"

Roger laughed like a machine gun. *Heheh. Heheheheh.*

Phil raised one eyebrow and shook his head. "I tell ya, Rita, my small-scale setup with the e-mails? Better than credit-card fraud. Low profile. The lonely ones'd give you anything just to *listen* to them for a few minutes. And with e-mail, you don't even have to do that! It's like, wow, nine pages about your childhood in Estonia. Delete!"

Sometimes when you dive headfirst into the deep end, life jumps in after you with a floaty thing and a glass of lemonade. When Brett looked at me, I knew what he was thinking.

Phil just said that out loud.

And, via live remote broadcast to Mrs. Skippy Chin's large-screen television, Federal Agent Hank Banazio had heard him.

"And that, folks, is what you call a colossal bust," said Money.

Brett refilled his cup of tea. "Rita is *excellent*, Claude."

"She should get an Oscar," said Lala.

Despite the fact that this was the second worst day of my life, I smiled. She was my true friend, Rita the Producer. And she could sell dirty water to a hot dog.

That's when I observed a man nearly as tall as the front window of the noodle shop running past it. Midrun he looked inside, saw Phil, and waved. Phil raised his hand, slowly, as Federal Agent Hank Banazio skidded into the shop and gave Mr. Chin a fist bump.

"Running late to an important appointment, Skip!" said Banazio, all out of breath. "But I didn't want to pass my favorite noodle shop without saying yo to my bros! What are you cats doing indoors this sunny afternoon? Brunch? You know, I miss those days at the Wharfman's Shore, Phil, enjoying a scalding-hot cup of that sludge you called coffee. What's with the suit? Coming from a funeral?"

Phil narrowed his eyes at Banazio.

I heard myself whisper, "No."

Mr. Chin glanced up at the one-way mirror. Then he said, "Nice seeing you as always, Hank. But I have some . . . soup to make . . ."

"Yep, me too, in the soup." Banazio slicked back his hair and turned to leave. He pointed at Dad. "That daughter of yours, Simon. Sharp as a fistful of razors! Don't worry, the USA won't let her down."

"No," I said. "No, no, *no*!"

"You know Claude, right, Philip?" said Banazio. "Had a deep talk with her the other day. Wow! I mean, *wow*." Then Banazio noticed Rita and froze. "Who's *that*?"

Rita looked around.

"What's going on, Claude?" asked Lala. "Do you know that guy too?"

Rita said, "I'm—"

Banazio interrupted her in a movie-star voice. "Single? I'm praying."

"LEAVE!" I yelled. "YOU'RE IN A HURRY!"

Banazio handed Rita his card.

"Hank Banazio, FBI. I'm in the middle of fighting a *large-scale, federal-level* crime right now, but I'll be free later, if you'd like to catch a drink? I know some great places around here. You can't find them in the guidebooks."

Rita's face made an expression I had never seen before, like she wanted to call an ambulance and crack up laughing at the same time.

"Is that guy part of the plan?" asked Money.

Banazio managed to remember he was in a hurry. He saluted the room and took off running down Eighth Avenue.

"Claude, who was that?" asked Brett, in a low, slow voice that told me he already knew the answer.

"That?" I said, as every cell in my body curled up to cry, "was the worst FBI agent in the world."

"I thought he was at Mr. Chin's house, watching Phil give it up?" said Money.

I felt Brett looking at me, but I couldn't look back. My heart was in my neck someplace, blocking traffic.

If Rita knew we'd just taken a nosedive into a toxic sinkhole, she didn't let on. She slid the paperwork and a pen to Phil and Roger. "Here's the contract. Don't hesitate to ask questions."

"Will the actress who plays me be hot?" asked Alma.

"Excellent question!" said Rita. "You'll appear very appropriate for a girl your age."

"What am I, eleven?" said Alma.

"I got a question, Rita," said Phil.

"Ask away!" said Rita.

Phil stood. "How dumb do you think I am?" He turned to Roger. "Lights out on this thing."

Alma leaned forward. "Excuse me? Phil? My show?" She wheeled around the table to Rita. "Lady! Write the check to my uh, friend, Joanie Gascogny—"

"Roger, shut her up," snapped Phil. The skin on his

face sagged as he walked around the table, holding out his hands like he was daring Dad to put something in them. "Something you wanna tell me, Simon? About Federal Agent Gotcha and some ideas bumpin' around that lump you call a head? Shame on you. Your father woulda been disgusted."

I had never seen my father snap.

Dad knocked over his chair and grabbed Phil by the shirt collar. Mr. Chin hopped over the counter yelling, "Si! Cool it!" Phil made like he was gonna throw a punch; Mr. Chin caught his arm and twisted it behind his back. Rita ran toward the cash register. Roger stumbled backward with both hands in front of his face, like he was afraid of getting socked. Alma twirled around in her wheelchair, laughing hysterically.

The last few customers left fast.

I ran through the kitchen with Brett, Lala, and Money right behind me and yelled, "PHIL!"

When our eyes met, the clock tower that looks out over Downtown Brooklyn stopped ticking, to give me time. Time to look at Phil and understand what he'd done. Time to know how things actually were, and feel how they actually felt.

Which was devastating.

Phil.

Phil?

Observing his silver hair, and his wrinkled face, I

felt a tear run down my cheek. When had it happened? When had Phil's heart gotten offed? I couldn't believe anybody'd be born that way. Heartless.

I made my voice as strong as I wanted to feel, even though I felt sad, very sad, and that was all.

"Give it up, Phil," I said. "You were trying to make money off people who wanted to help a sick little girl. But this girl ain't little and she ain't sick. It's pathetic."

Phil's eyes reminded me of one of those wild dogs that prowl the edges of the Gowanus Canal, fighting for scraps. But he couldn't look at me for long. He talked to the ceiling, to the fluorescent lights. "I coulda used you, Claude. Business is always expanding. Just had to toughen you up a little bit. You girls. You get so sensitive."

And as he talked to the ceiling instead of me, I swore I caught a glimpse of the person I thought I knew still fighting with this other Phil—Phil the liar, Phil the thief. Maybe, just maybe, his heart wasn't quite dead yet. Maybe it was leaving him messages with every beat, and he told himself he'd get back to it, someday.

Phil tried to yank his arms away from Mr. Chin. "Simon, tell this goon to lemme go. Unless you want me announcing to the neighborhood that you got a friend downtown."

For a split second I was distracted. *People really say that?*

Dad didn't look comfortable-uncomfortable. He

looked straight-up nervous. "Good idea, Phil," he said. "Go."

Mr. Chin loosened his grip. Roger grabbed Alma's wheelchair and whirled it to face the door.

Lala grabbed my wrist and whispered. "This can't be it. Phil confessed!"

"Claude?" said Rita.

Brett looked at me like he wanted to do something but he didn't know what.

I wasn't sure what to do either.

On their way to the door, Phil turned back. "You know who I keep thinkin' about, Claudeline?"

"I don't know anything about you, anymore, Phil," I said.

"Your grandfather. Him?" Phil pointed at Dad. "Him, Si had no hope for. But you? Reason he woke up in the morning. To think his granddaughter would go the rat route? Kills me. Just as well he ain't around to see it."

That's when somebody else turned up in the noodle shop. Somebody wearing a light-blue wrap dress with a gold belt and bronze high heels.

THE ANGEL NIECE

Miss Piggy: *I spy because I care!*
Kermit the Frog: *Well, I care too!*
Miss Piggy: *Well, why don't you say so?*
Kermit the Frog: *I JUST DID!*
Miss Piggy: *ALL RIGHT!*
—*The Muppets Take Manhattan*, movie

The hot light from the street made Mom's bleached hair and metallic accessories shimmer like she was radioactive, and she was shooting Phil with the fattest eye-laser-beam death ray I'd ever seen outside an intergalactic war movie with a massive special-effects budget. "Get away from my daughter," she said, all out of breath.

Phil laughed quietly.

"Sara?" said Dad.

"If it ain't my little angel niece," said Phil.

"I told you, *step back*," snapped Mom. "And can it with the niece thing. It grosses me out."

As Alma ducked under her lap blanket, Dad ran to Mom and stretched his arm in front of her like a seat belt. "You wanna tell me what's going on, Sara?"

"Phil and his slimeball brother are finally going to jail," said Mom.

Phil's sunken eye sockets were pools of shadows. "Somebody's feelin' full of herself," he said.

"I kept your frauds a secret for twenty years," said Mom. "You repay me by messing with my kid? How dare you."

"Mom, what are you talking about?" I said.

"Don't worry, Sara," said Phil. "Uncle Phil knows you ain't told nobody nothin' about nothin'. Who'd believe you?"

"Who do you think believes me?" said Mom. "Said he's working something in the neighborhood and nobody go nowhere till he gets here." She rubbed her heel where her shoe was cutting in. "Late, as usual. Somebody get that ape a watch."

"What'd ya tell Gotcha, Sara?" asked Phil. "About that real estate business you ran with me all those years, up in the Bronx?"

"*What?*" said Dad and me, at the same time.

Mom pointed at Phil. "You tellin' a nine-year-old girl to play sick, stickin' me in the corner of some room to distract people while you sold 'em buildings that were rotten from the outside in, and givin' my father a cut? Nobody who's not you would call that *running a business together*."

The empty smile on Phil's hollow face made my skin

prickle. "Your mother was a natural, Claude. Another reason I had hope for you. But she ain't a rat. Not Sara."

So many questions were swarming my head, I started spitting stuff out at random. "Phil has been running scams for *twenty years*? He stuck you in a *corner*? Mom, why have you never told me this?! And how did you even know we were here?"

"Your e-mail said Sunday, noon," said Mom. "Where else would you be?"

I yelled, "You broke into my e-mail?!"

That's when Banazio strutted into the noodle shop and danced a jig. "Gotcha! *Gotcha.*" The room was flooded with the fuzzy sound of walkie-talkies as three cops rushed in behind him. "Hank Banazio," he announced, waving his badge. "FBI."

"Fancy seein' ya, Gotcha," said Phil, backing away from the police officer who was coming toward him. "As per the usual, hate to disappoint you . . ."

"Who's disappointed?" said Banazio. "Oh—wait. I forgot to say it, right? Phil and Roger Gascogny, you're under arrest."

The cops slapped handcuffs on Phil and Roger—who were, apparently, brothers, not brothers-in-law—and walked them to the back of the shop, reading them their rights, just like on *Law & Order*.

I yelled, "How can they be under arrest, Banazio? You missed the entire bust!"

Banazio made a clicking noise with his tongue. "Sorry about that. Sun's been so rare this drippy summer, I was parked on a bench, basking, and oops! *Hank, you're late!* To think I proceeded to stumble into the midst of the action, not knowing what tomfoolery was afoot. Then I get to Eleventh Avenue, and it's like, the place is nowhere to be found. That address you gave me, C-Feng, it's kind of hidden, right?"

"Nope," said Mr. Chin, taking a seat at a table. "My doorbell is clearly marked."

"Nevertheless. There I am, searching for the hidden address, when lo and behold, my telephone rings! And after all these years, who's come a-callin'? The Hellcat. If you hadn't set these fellas up, C-Feng? Your mother never would've buzzed me. Turns out these yokesters have been running illegal moneymaking operations in this city for as many years as I've been trying to convince Sara 'the Hellcat' LeBernardin to talk to me. The Hellcat knows all! Little did I know that the power of maternal love was the one thing that could make her spill the beans. Beautiful. Next summer, C-Feng, see me about an internship. You and all your gangster pals, too."

"Maybe *you* should intern with *us*, FBI guy," said Lala.

Banazio peered at Lala. "Yowza. She's a quick one. And speaking of wow . . ." He spun on his heel to face Rita, who was standing near the cops and the handcuffed Gascogny brothers, taking notes. When she stuck her tongue between her teeth and waved, her silver tooth flashed. Banazio strolled smoothly in her direction.

I looked at Mom. "You knew Phil was Alma the whole time?"

Mom pulled a brush out of her purse and started messing with my hair for the first time since I was about five years old. "Oh, Claude. I've always known way too much. Unfortunately. Tell you the details later. I'm all talked out." Then she looked over her shoulder and noticed the wheelchair, which was near the cash register. The blanket still covered Alma's head, but her long legs stuck out, frozen, like a Halloween lawn decoration. Mom snorted. "When'd you get outta the pen, Joanie?"

A voice beneath the blanket went, *"Shhh!"*

Mom muttered to herself while she worked through my tangles. "Breaking parole, are we, Joanie Maloney? Gascogny now, which figures. Soon as I deal with my ragamuffin's head of hair, I will report you, too, you lunatic."

Mom must've been in too much of a rush to put on her makeup. Her dark blue eyes were clear, like somebody'd flipped on the power, and her sea of orangey freckles made me think of one of those storybook girls who talks to lions and bears.

I felt myself bust out with a huge smile. "You broke into my e-mail, Mom," I said. "That means you actually care."

When Mom pinched my cheek, I yelped. A storybook girl with the gentle touch of a lobster, that is.

"Of course I care, Claude," said Mom. "I love you. Or, you know. Yeah."

It had been so long since I'd seen Mom smile, I'd forgotten all about her crooked teeth.

When I hugged her, I inhaled a salty breeze.

"I love you too, Mom," I said. "Nice nickname, by the way."

"Nobody has *ever* called me 'the Hellcat,'" said Mom.

I said, still squeezing her, "And nobody's gonna start now."

Living in New York City is like having your very own eight-million-headed dog. Sometimes it brings you strange gifts, like a musician on the N train who makes you dance in your seat, or a practically perfect shawarma with garlic sauce, and you'd swear all its faces are smiling at you. Other times it barks all night and pees on your favorite shoes.

That afternoon, the dog trotted along with Mom, Dad, and me like part of the family. The heat rising up off Eighth Avenue caught the sunlight and pitched it here and there, at the cars and the shop windows, making twinkles, and curled around us, friendly, as we rounded the corner to walk down Sixtieth Street, toward home. Lala and Money had left the noodle shop on his scooter, and Brett had stayed behind to get the sesame ice cream for his mother. I'd promised to join him for old-timey movies later.

Dad was shaking his head. "I wish you'd told me you and Phil went back like that, Sara."

"I wish you'd told me you were sending his fake sick girl money," said Mom.

"This whole family gets triple Fs in communication," I said. "Seriously, Mom, if you've always known Phil was a creep, why did you keep quiet about it? The man was practically my babysitter!"

Mom clasped her hands behind her back and looked ahead of us, like she was walking toward something she'd been thinking about, which at the same time was pulling her forward. "My whole life, Claude, I was supposed to act like I couldn't see things. Bad things that were happening right in front of me. It's hard to unlearn that, and speak up. It feels unnatural. Like the whole world works one way, and your world works a different way. And the outside world might not want you in it, or you wouldn't know how to be in it, if it did. You end up trusting the people you know and *don't* trust more than the people you don't know at all. I always figured that by keeping Phil close, I'd never have another problem with him. It sounds ridiculous when I say it out loud. When he started up with another sick-girl scam, I did try to keep you away—but you're not accustomed to being told what to do. Thankfully, in addition to being stubborn, you've got more courage than me. I'm sorry, Claude. Nobody's born a parent. I'm learning by screwing up."

I tried to imagine being a parent. If it was anything like being a kid, it was not a slice of vanilla birthday cake with a smear of buttercream and a mess of sugar flowers you can eat right off the top. As far as I could tell, nothing was, except actual cake. Which was what was so great about it.

"Why does Phil call you his niece?" I asked.

"Phil has always wanted to be a gangster," said Mom. "He wanted it so bad he started pretending we were related. He even kept a picture of me in his wallet. Flashed it around when he was tryin' to soften up some guy for the kill."

Was that *Mom*, in the photo Phil showed me? How had I not recognized her?

"Why don't I ever see pictures of when you were a kid?" I asked.

"My childhood isn't something I go around trying to remember," said Mom.

"Yeah, because nobody thought about your feelings at all," I said. "No wonder you're so mean sometimes."

Mom started laughing. Laughing and snorting.

"SO MEAN!" I said. "Right? Because so many people were mean to you?"

When Dad put his arm around Mom, he looked like

a grown-up, real-life parent, even with the blue stripe. "Speaking of mean, lemme put it out there how lucky Phil is that my pop wasn't here to see this. If Grandpa thought somebody was messing with you, Claude? Guarantee he wouldn't have asked Gotcha to deal with it."

"I miss Grandpa," I said. "Even if he *was* a bad guy, I miss him twice as bad."

"We all do," said Mom. "I even miss my own parents. Wish somebody'd help me make sense of that one."

"It makes sense to us, Mom," I said.

Dad frowned and gave Mom's shoulder a squeeze. "No doubt."

SUNSET PARK

The spider is a repairer. If you bash into the web of a spider, she doesn't get mad. She weaves and she repairs it.
—Louise Bourgeois, artist

After Alma Lingonberry, life in Sunset Park kept going and going, like a shopping cart full of junk let loose on a downhill avenue.

Brett and I decided I'd put my photograph of the Fuzhou crew in my closet. I wanted to keep it, just not on my wall. I didn't want to watch the Thing hanging out with my grandfather like it was a friend that would protect him. Because it didn't. If Grandpa was here, I think he'd be glad I'm a few steps ahead of him, as usual. I'm tap-dancing, even. Leading my past, and my parents' pasts, and their parents' pasts in a never-ending parade around the planet. Like we all are.

Like Brett is. His new project is a philosophy newsletter for parents stuck in prison. He took up Banazio on his offer of an FBI internship and is using his new connections to get it out. He doesn't let things go, my best friend. It's one of the things I love most about him.

Lala and Money broke up for five seconds when Money said he missed pretending to be Scott Jones, with all those friends—but they made up five seconds later, when he recited one of her poems by heart. Yes, he'd gotten that poem by spying on her e-mails to Alma, but as they say in Brooklyn in the movies, *Whaddayagonnadoaboudit?*

Rita the Producer moved to Los Angeles with her new boyfriend to try to sell her screenplay. "Hank Banazio makes me laugh" is what she told me. "And he doesn't hog the spotlight. That's a rare specimen, Claudeline."

Which reminds me of what Brett said when we were hanging out on our bench in the park, analyzing how the doofus FBI agent snagged a snazzy dame like Rita.

"Who knows?" said Brett. "Chapter seventeen says that a great leader keeps a low profile. When the task is completed, the people say, 'We did it ourselves.'"

"We did do it ourselves," I said. "Banazio wasn't our leader at all!"

Brett nudged me. "I meant *you*, Claude. You were our leader. Banazio was one of the people. Anyway, we don't do anything all by ourselves, in my opinion. Everything in the world is connected. All the good things that happen, and all the bad things too."

Speaking of this tangled-up web of a world, I guess I'll probably always miss Phil. It's not like I want to spend time with the guy. It's the old version I miss. Laughing with him. Or maybe it's the old days I miss, when I didn't think too hard about stuff. Anyway, even if I could go back to those days, I wouldn't want to.

Neither does Mom. She told me that when Phil went to jail, Chef Guillaume cried, and not because his fancy-schmancy restaurant lost its *authenticity*. Phil had been robbing him, and Guillaume had been too scared to do anything about it. But even with Phil gone, Mom quit. She said she wanted to try her luck in the world outside the one she'd always known. The bartender at her new restaurant, he's pleasant enough, but he's always yappin' about law school and the stock market and the yadda yadda.

With no Phil and no Rita, I don't go into Manhattan much anymore. Nowadays me, Brett, and Lala—and Money, when we can drag him into the daylight—spend our free time at the noodle shop, hanging out with Dad.

I'm gonna leave you with the words Skippy Chin said when he handed Dad the keys to the noodle shop so he could retire with his wife in their house over on Eleventh Avenue.

"Remember, Si," said Mr. Chin, "you're only as good or as bad as your last bowl of noodles."

At least I think that's what he said. Anyway, as far as philosophies go, I think that's pretty easy to swallow.

As far as stories? Why not go with the happy ending.

—C. LeB., Sunset Park, Brooklyn

AFTERWORD: HOW I PICKED MY PHILOSOPHY

Lao Tzu is the Chinese philosopher Brett is obsessed with. That summer, Brett was carrying around a book the guy wrote more than two thousand years ago called the *Tao Te Ching*. The librarian with the turquoise hair told me it's been translated from ancient Chinese hundreds of times, and every time, the words come out a little different.

I gotta give that librarian a shout-out. Every time I asked her a question, such as "Who are some philosophers?" or "How do you tell a detective story?" she stuck a book in my hands. She didn't just give me so-called kids' books either. Even if I didn't understand everything in those books, there was usually at least one part that made sense. Now whenever I come across something I like, I add it to my philosophy collection.

So that's the philosophy of my philosophy. Now I've REALLY got nothin' left to say, so I'm gonna do this:

Withdraw as soon as your work is done.

—Lao Tzu

ACKNOWLEDGMENTS

I'd like to thank my agent, Susan Hawk, and my editor, Kristin Ostby, for believing in this novel from the start, and for working so diligently to make it great. Thanks to the entire team at Simon & Schuster, including Laurent Linn and Mekisha Telfer, for their enthusiasm, and for the creativity with which they have handled each stage of the production process. Ziyue Chen's warm and cheerful cover illustration captures the sunset tone of the story perfectly. My husband, Tim Mapp, my son, Laszlo, and my stepdaughter, Adèle, are sources of love, encouragement, and inspiration. I am also indebted to the many readers and friends who gave this book, and me, the utmost care and consideration over the past several years: Ginny Wiehardt, Lisa Thornton, Ron Horning, Anna West, Andy Dowdy, Matt Weedman, Katherine Leggett, Leslie Robarge, Lhasa Ray, Susan Levin, Jeffrey Yang, Michelle Alumkal, Colie Collen, Adriana X. Jacobs, David Jacobs, Jonathan Regier, Jennifer K. Dick, Jacob Bromberg,

ACKNOWLEDGMENTS

Cynthia Tolentino, Edith Balbach, Todd Fletcher, Mei Ying So, Lee O'Connor, Yael Lehmann, Xiaoyu Sun, and Shuk Yi Wong. Megan, Alex, Amaya, and Luca Zesati, Kyla Krug-Meadows, and the indefatigable infant and toddler teachers at Lucasfilm cared for my newborn, my husband, and me so lovingly while I revised; we owe you our sanity. Rob Liguori provided swift, skilled fact-checking at a critical moment. The errors that remain are my own. I'd also like to thank the Rees family, for years of kindness, and my family, especially Barbara Balbach-Haines, David Lariviere, Geraldine Tierney, Sarah and Stanley Balbach, Allane and Louis Lariviere, and Pat and Jim Mapp. Finally, thank you to all the families and students with whom I have had the pleasure of working in my capacities as a clinical social worker and as an instructor. Every story is connected.